MY HERO ACADEMIA

SCHOOL BRIEFS

3

Dorm Days

ORIGINAL CONCEPT BY
KOHEI HORIKOSHI

WRITTEN BY
ANRI YOSHI

U.A. HIGH SCHOOL

Hero Course: Class 1-A

Izuku Midoriya

Birthday: July 15
Quirk: One For All

Katsuki Bakugo

Birthday: April 20
Quirk: Explosion

Shoto Todoroki

Birthday: January 11
Quirk:
Half-Cold Half-Hot

Tenya Ida

Birthday: August 22
Quirk: Engine

Fumikage Tokoyami

Birthday: October 30
Quirk: Dark Shadow

Minoru Mineta

Birthday: October 8
Quirk: Pop Off

Ochaco Uraraka

Birthday:
December 27
Quirk: Zero Gravity

Momo Yaoyorozu

Birthday:
September 23
Quirk: Creation

Tsuyu Asui

Birthday: February 12
Quirk: Frog

Yuga Aoyama

Birthday: May 30
Quirk: Navel Laser

Mina Ashido

Birthday: July 30
Quirk: Acid

Mashirao Ojiro

Birthday: May 28
Quirk: Tail

Denki Kaminari

Birthday: June 29
Quirk: Electrification

Eijiro Kirishima

Birthday: October 16
Quirk: Hardening

Koji Koda

Birthday: February 1
Quirk: Anivoice

Rikido Sato

Birthday: June 19
Quirk: Sugar Rush

Mezo Shoji

Birthday: February 15
Quirk: Dupli-Arms

Kyoka Jiro

Birthday: August 1
Quirk: Earphone Jack

Hanta Sero

Birthday: July 28
Quirk: Tape

Toru Hagakure

Birthday: June 16
Quirk: Invisibility

Hero Course: Class 1-B

Itsuka Kendo

Birthday:
September 9
Quirk: Big Fist

Neito Monoma

Birthday: May 13
Quirk: Copy

Tetsutetsu Tetsutetsu

Birthday: October 16
Quirk: Steel

Pony Tsunotori

Birthday: April 21
Quirk: Horn Cannon

Hero Course: Faculty

All Might

Birthday: June 10
Quirk: One For All

Shota Aizawa

Birthday: November 8
Quirk: Erasure

Thirteen

Birthday: February 3
Quirk: Black Hole

Cementoss

Birthday: March 22
Quirk: Cement

Midnight

Birthday: March 9
Quirk: Somnambulist

Ectoplasm

Birthday: March 23
Quirk: Clones

Present Mic

Birthday: July 7
Quirk: Voice

Vlad King

Birthday:
November 10
Quirk: Blood Control

MY HERO ACADEMIA

SCHOOL BRIEFS

3

CONTENTS

Dorm Days

Part 1
Cheers

Near U.A. High School, Shota Aizawa led All Might to a back-alley *izakaya* started by a former faculty member of the U.A. Business Course. The well-worn *noren* curtain facing the alley bore the name of the establishment—Sanzaru, meaning "three monkeys"—and just behind it stood a ratty sliding door that promised cheap eats within. Ducking past the curtain and through the door revealed just the sort of hole one might expect to find down an alley, with a counter that seated five or six and a few standard tables. Nestled off to the side was a low table for customers who preferred sitting on the floor, on tatami mats, with an alcove featuring a *daruma* and other typical izakaya decorations.

It was only a bit past opening time, which probably explained why the place was empty. The smiling yet taciturn proprietor invited All Might and Aizawa to take the low table, and they did so, sitting down opposite each other. Within minutes, they had appetizers, drinks, and bone-shaped chopstick holders in front of them. As a nondrinker, All Might had ordered nonalcoholic beer, while Aizawa got a glass of the real stuff.

"How about a toast?" said All Might. His right arm was bound in a cast, so his left held the glass aloft.

"To what, exactly?" asked Aizawa, making his companion stop and think.

"To a successful round of home visits, let's say."

The training camp earlier that summer had been meant to prepare the students to test for their provisional hero licenses, but everything had gone awry when the League of Villains had attacked and kidnapped Katsuki Bakugo. A few days later, heroes and law enforcement came together to organize a pair of raids designed to rescue Bakugo and put an end to the league, and the operation ended with a brutal battle between All Might and the league's mastermind, the man known only as All For One. All Might's Quirk, "One For All," had been passed down through the generations in order to one day defeat All For One, but since All Might had already given it to Izuku Midoriya, he'd had to fight this final battle with what few embers remained within him. The clash left him drained of his former might, forcing him to announce his retirement from his position as top hero.

Though the wicked mastermind was now in prison, his successor—Tomura Shigaraki—and the rest of the League of Villains had slipped through the authorities' fingers. All For One had revealed during the battle that Shigaraki was in fact the grandson of All Might's own master, which gave the hero more than a little pause. Despite this, he'd resolved to focus on the task at hand—raising Midoriya to be the next Symbol of Peace.

Though safety and security for its students had always been a priority, the recent events had prompted U.A. High to step up its game by implementing a dormitory system. The faculty also hoped this change would allow them to identify a potential mole who had been leaking intel to the villains.

During the home visits they'd made that day, All Might and Aizawa had explained the dorm system to the parents while formally asking permission for the school to look after their children in a greater capacity. At one point during the day, All Might had promised to buy Aizawa a drink.

U.A

"Anyhow, cheers!"

"Good work today."

Their glasses clinked, and it was down the hatch with the chilled beers. Nothing quite like that cold fizz at the end of a summer's day. All Might had newfound resolve about his role as an educator, so it was on days like this one that he wished he could still drink the hard stuff. As he placed his glass down, he was shocked to find that Aizawa was still going at it; by the time Aizawa slammed his own glass onto the table with a satisfied "Phew," it was completely empty.

"You don't hold back, do you, Aizawa? Fond of booze, I take it?"

"No more than anyone else."

All Might reached for the large bottle to pour Aizawa another, but the latter said, "Don't bother. Easier for me to," before filling his glass for a second time. It suddenly dawned on All Might that he and Aizawa had never been alone like this before, so why not take advantage?

These two didn't exactly see eye to eye. While Aizawa lived by the law of rationality, All Might was always going above and beyond as the Symbol of Peace, providing a little more than anyone asked for. But now Aizawa was class 1-A's homeroom teacher, with All Might as his official backup, so of course it'd make more sense if they could communicate and get along. All Might figured that alcohol was just the thing to relax Aizawa's rational ways and break down the wall guarding his inner thoughts.

Today's the day I really become friends with Aizawa!

With clenched fists, All Might turned his thoughts to this goal—finding a topic they could bond over.

"You come here often?" asked All Might.

"Now and then," replied his tight-lipped companion.

"Sure, sure. Any recommendations from the menu?"

"Um... I never eat much here. Should we order something for you?"

"Ah, that's all right. I don't eat much in general."

Aizawa had managed to drain his glass again during this uneventful exchange. He poured himself some more and finished it just as quickly.

"You never told me you're such a hard drinker, Aizawa."

"I'm not, really."

Huh? He still seems perfectly sober?

All Might flashed a friendly smile but tilted his head in puzzlement. Even with three whole glasses of beer in him, Aizawa was his usual detached self. He drank so nonchalantly that All Might wondered if the proprietor hadn't accidentally brought a bottle of nonalcoholic stuff.

"That's real beer, right?" said All Might, checking the bottle's label.

"Obviously."

"Do you not get drunk, then?"

"I don't remember ever getting drunk," said Aizawa after a brief pause.

So the guy can handle his liquor. All Might was still

convinced that a drunk Aizawa would be more open to friendship, so he encouraged his companion to keep pounding them back. Aizawa obliged.

"Tell me—what do you do on your days off, Aizawa?"

"I sleep."

"Any TV shows you're into lately?"

"Not really."

"I hear that a good hot compress does wonders for dry eye!"

"I'm aware."

With a rigid, strained smile on his face, All Might racked his brain. Aizawa seemed no different than usual, but "usual" meant being at school, surrounded by noise and action. In stark contrast, the izakaya proprietor said nothing and no cars rumbled past in the alley outside, so when the two heroes' conversation flatlined, an awkward silence settled over the place. Meanwhile, Aizawa showed no signs of inebriation. Maybe he never would. Maybe he'd only agreed to come on the spur of the moment but was already regretting it. Clearly not interested in conversation, Aizawa just kept drinking.

Oh lord…

No villain could make All Might flinch, but a spot of awkwardness was enough to make him crumple. It'd been too much to expect that he and Aizawa would be instant friends, especially since his companion was likely also aware how much their outlooks on life differed. But a memory from earlier in the day suddenly popped into All Might's mind.

"Because I'm gonna be a hero!"

That had been Midoriya's declaration to his mother when she'd seemed ready to withdraw him from school. The boy was willing to sacrifice U.A. as long he could still attend another school with a hero course.

I can't give up either!

All Might was determined to support his brave little successor, who never stopped pursuing his dreams. What sort of mentor would he be if a little awkwardness stopped him in his tracks? Besides, from the moment he'd decided to go drinking with Aizawa, All Might had had a certain question on his mind. It wasn't one that would necessarily lead to friendship, but it felt just as important. All Might cleared his throat and spoke.

"Can I ask you something, Aizawa?"

"What is it now?"

"Do you have any tips for teaching? Or a way to get in the right frame of mind, as an educator?"

Aizawa squinted and furrowed his brow, as if he'd just been accused of having two heads. All Might hastily went on.

"Since I'm still so new to this teaching gig, I mean."

Since All Might had questions about a profession, why not ask a professional? Though Aizawa was no charmer, he'd already earned the trust of twenty impressionable adolescents, so All Might was hoping to emulate the man's approach to education. In a two-birds-one-stone sense, shoptalk might also be the thing to help them bond.

All Might was ready for an answer, but Aizawa remained silent.

"Aizawa?"

The taciturn teacher scratched at his cheek, seemingly annoyed.

"If there are tips out there, I wish someone would tell me. We're dealing with a whole set of different personalities and backgrounds, each growing at different rates. If there were a quick and easy instruction manual for this job, society would've been villain-free a long time ago."

Aizawa had been an educator for years, so the weight of his words hit All Might hard.

"Right. Of course..." said All Might. He shrank a bit, visibly ashamed that he'd been hoping for shortcuts at a job as important as this. He'd even been planning to look for how-to books on the way home, thinking the answers would be easily laid out for him.

"You're saying it's important to recognize each student as an individual, right? I'm routinely shocked by how fast those boys and girls seem to grow. In fact, one who's always walked in my shadow seems to be setting his own course lately..." All Might was still looking deflated, but a hint of joy glinted in his eyes as he sipped his drink. Listening in silence, Aizawa shot him a suspicious look.

"And who might that be?"

"Huh?" said All Might, lifting his head. The student he had in mind was, of course, Midoriya.

"I've been meaning to say something, actually."

"Really, now? I'm open to any and all advice!"

"About Midoriya."

At the sound of his mentee's name, All Might's heart

MY HERO ACADEMIA SCHOOL BRIEFS

nearly stopped, and it took every ounce of willpower to keep a straight face.

"W-what about Midoriya, exactly?"

"I don't think you should play favorites the way you do."

"N-no, it's not like that…"

"He's got a similar Quirk to yours, and he puts in the effort to match, so I get your interest in him. Educators are human, too. But you can't let that show so much. That sort of bias is antithetical to your role as a teacher."

Midoriya's Quirk wasn't just similar—he had the exact same Quirk that All Might had once possessed, though All Might couldn't very well come out and tell Aizawa that. Besides, Aizawa wasn't wrong; successor and mentee or not, Midoriya shouldn't be getting special treatment from a member of the U.A. faculty. All Might suddenly doubted himself, wondering if he'd been shortchanging his other students.

"Yes, you're right…" he said, shrinking even more, like a schoolboy scolded by a teacher.

We'll never get chummy at this rate!

The cloud of awkwardness hanging over the room had only grown.

"Also..." began Aizawa, but his ringing phone cut him off.

"Heya! MC Mic is crashing the 1-A teachers' secret get-together! Start me off with a beer, Chief! Hang on—'start me off'? That seems a little rude to the beer, considering it's about to keep me company!"

After hearing about the rendezvous on the phone from Aizawa, it hadn't taken Present Mic even five minutes to show up and plop himself down next to his colleague, who hadn't technically extended an invitation.

"What's up with that, giving me the cold shoulder? You're s'posed to let me know whenever you're going drinking!"

"Leave."

"One-word answer? Brrr, man, brrr! That shoulder's positively icy! Hey, Chief, how about some piping hot yakitori skewers to raise the temp over here! Salt flavor!

Might as well toss in some *morokyu*, *shiokara*, and *karaage* too!"

Present Mic's show-stopping appearance livened the place up instantly, making a more relaxed All Might breathe a sigh of relief. Aizawa and Mic had been classmates themselves, so they already got along, so to speak.

Mic's beer showed up soon after he bellowed out the order, and he raised his glass in a toast.

"Knocking back a cold one after work is my idea of heaven, boys! You two make for an odd couple, though— like oil and water! Manage to do any mixing yet?"

Argh! Don't make a point of it!

All Might panicked, since Mic was never one for delicacy around sensitive issues. The sharp-eyed Mic noticed All Might's discomfort and grinned.

"Oh? Try to mix oil and water, and they just stay separate, huh? This's why you shoulda invited me from the start, since I'm the kinda guy who can liven up any party! And hey, ain't this our first time sharing drinks, All Might?"

"I believe it is, yes."

There'd been talks of a welcome party for All Might

at the start of the school year, but circumstances just hadn't allowed for it. The food arrived, and All Might asked Mic a question while picking at his plate.

"Do you go drinking with Aizawa much?"

"Sometimes! I invite this guy out plenty enough, but he's a tough nut to crack!"

"Who could possibly go drinking that often? I'd rather spend my Sundays doing nothing," said Aizawa, butting in.

"What are days off for, if not hangovers?"

"Literally anything else."

"You gotta do some irrational stuff once in a while, buddy!"

The sight of Mic egging on his apathetic friend was a common one in the staff room at school, but throwing alcohol into the mix only seemed to dial it up several notches. Somehow, though, Aizawa actually looked more relaxed than earlier, meaning that Present Mic had managed what All Might had not. He'd have to watch and learn from this performance.

"You two were in the same year at U.A., right? Mind if I ask how you became friends, despite your, er, differences?"

Mic gave an enthusiastic nod.

"Right, sure! Well, my friend here never seemed to have much to say, so I figured it was my job to chat him up and loosen his nerves!"

"I was never nervous," grumbled Aizawa, sipping his beer and still apparently stone-cold sober.

Paying the quip no mind, Mic went on. "Given how little he talked, I was convinced he was a robot made to look like a real boy! Plus, he'd always snooze during breaks between classes. He's all about doing the bare minimum, right? So for a while, our classmates took to calling him 'Power-Saver Sho'! Ain't that right, Sho?"

Aizawa's eyes popped open wide, and before All Might knew it, Aizawa had Present Mic in a sleeper hold.

"Urk!"

"You're the one who started that nickname...among plenty of other inane ones..."

"Right, like 'Prince of Slumberland,' a.k.a. 'P.O.S.'! Or how about 'Snooze Master'?"

As Present Mic recounted the insulting nicknames fondly, Aizawa tightened his grip without a moment's hesitation.

"Not another word."

"Not too tight now, Aizawa!" blurted All Might.

"This is the only way to get him to stop blabbing."

"Uncle, uncle! I give!"

But Mic's cry fell on deaf ears, as Aizawa seemed determined to put his colleague down for a nap of his own. Not wanting to see one pro hero knock out another, All Might was preparing to intervene when the door to the izakaya rattled open.

"Evening, Chief... Oh? All Might? Eraser? Mic?"

"What's going on over there?"

It was Midnight and Thirteen. Though Midnight was in civilian clothes, Thirteen still wore his usual space suit.

"H-help..." croaked Mic.

"I'm guessing Mic didn't know when to shut up? He reaps what he sows, I say," shot back Midnight, clearly used to walking in on such scenes.

"No, no, no! We oughtn't make trouble in public!" said Thirteen.

Aizawa released his grip as his conscientious colleague's point struck a chord. Mic explained the whole thing to the two newcomers, who joined the

table. Midnight sat to Mic's right, while Thirteen took a seat next to All Might.

"I'll have the usual, Chief! And tea for you, Thirteen? Just like always?"

"Yes, thank you... Actually, on second thought, why don't I indulge today?"

Thirteen ordered a lemon sour, prompting a quizzical look from Midnight.

"You never drink, though."

"All Might is with us today, making this a special occasion indeed," said Thirteen, probably beaming under his space helmet. As their little drinking party grew even livelier, All Might started feeling less and less awkward.

"I'm thrilled to get to drink with you all, even if I can't really drink, so to speak! I have to ask, though— aren't you uncomfortable in that suit, Thirteen?"

"I'm far more comfortable this way, actually," replied Thirteen as he removed his helmet and placed it to the side in anticipation of food and drink.

"Got the lemon sour and...tequila, here," said the proprietor, setting the drinks on the table.

"Your usual is *tequila*, Midnight?"

Another toast prompted Midnight to take a swig of her drink, impressing All Might.

"You're clearly a strong drinker, Midnight."

"Oh? But I've only got a taste for the stuff that really sets my gut on fire."

"That's U.A.'s biggest boozehound for ya! If only she weren't such an obnoxious drunk!"

"Obnoxious? How so?" asked All Might, shocked by Mic's declaration.

"If you don't shut up, Mic, you're going to find yourself pickled like one of those tequila worms," said a glowering Midnight before taking another gulp of her drink.

"Do it. For all our sakes," muttered Aizawa between sips of beer.

"What kinda friend sells out a friend, friend?" said Mic. "You forgetting who came up with 'Eraser Head'? Your old pal here gave you that cooler-than-cool hero code name!"

"If that means I owe you some sort of debt, I'll pick another name."

"How about P.O.S.?"

"Shut. Up."

Aizawa went for a standard headlock this time, which had Mic crying "I give, I give!" in no time at all. Midnight didn't lift a finger to intervene, but she did shake her head as if rejecting an idea.

"No, '100 Proof Mic' would probably just be the wrong sort of party in your mouth."

"Oh yeah? What would I taste like, d'you think?"

All Might fretted, unsure if it was his place to say anything. At his side, Thirteen finished a sip of his lemon sour and spoke.

"Um, you're fond of Yakushima cedar trees, aren't you, All Might? I'm a nature lover myself, and I often watch nature documentaries! In fact, I've been wanting to talk to you about those cedars for a while now!"

"You should've spoken up sooner! I always welcome a talk with someone who understands what makes those trees so great! Nothing can match their sense of majesty, I say!"

"Agreed! Their incredible vitality borders on the divine."

"There is something sacred about them, isn't there? Overwhelming yet inviting...and always leaving me oh so inspired to try harder."

Thirteen made an unexpected face.

"You clearly feel the same way I do, All Might, and I had a feeling we might find common ground over this. I, too, feel inspired when watching those documentaries... Oh, speaking of, have you had a chance to catch *Yakushima Cedars: Life in Perpetuity*?"

"Oh, was that one that they aired? I must've missed it!"

"Yes, it was incredible! Shall I make a copy for you?"

"Would you? Much appreciated!"

Each man gripped his drink in one hand while the passionate conversation about trees went on, and before he knew it, All Might had already forgotten about the earlier awkwardness between him and Aizawa.

I never imagined I'd find someone so willing to chat about Yakushima cedars... Maybe this outing wasn't a mistake after all?

The excitement over this shared interest got Thirteen riled, leading him to drain his lemon sour all the faster. By the time All Might realized that his fellow nature lover was acting odd, it was too late.

"Nature'sh jusht, like, sho amazing! We couldn't even breathe without nature, y'know? Tell me y'get it too, All Might?"

"Th-Thirteen, I think that drink's gone to your head! Here, have some water…"

"Water! That'sh another one of nature'sh great giftsh! Nope. Won't drink it. Don't desherve it. Tell me your thoughtsh about water, All Might."

Thirteen was tripping over his words at full throttle, leaving All Might feeling cornered and flustered.

"I-I think we ought to treat water like the precious resource it is…?"

"Shure, but how? I want shpecificsh."

"Um, M-Midnight!"

Midnight responded to All Might's call for rescue with a bewitching smile.

"Thirteen happens to be a clingy drunk."

"You could've mentioned that earlier!"

"Only didn't because we were all here having a good time already. Anyway, here, All Might… Wait. You can't drink. Ah, Eraser—drink this."

The glass in Midnight's outstretched hand held a dingy fluid. While All Might had been otherwise occupied, she'd gotten her hands on several more drinks whose empty glasses now littered the table.

"What is that, Midnight?" asked All Might,

struggling to peel a very attached Thirteen off of him.

"Just making cocktails out of other cocktails. The ones straight off the menu are so boooring, y'know? Booze is just like life—bound to get dull without spice, adventure, and new experiences. So here, Eraser, I've got a new taste sensation just for you."

"No. I've already got a drink," said Aizawa with a scowl.

"Such a bore. Are you like this in bed, too?"

"Bed? I prefer a sleeping bag."

"This is Midnight's drunken Quirk, All Might! She mixes up nasty cocktails and tries to pour 'em down our throats!" explained Present Mic.

"I drink them too, though. Finding out what they taste like is such a thrill! Wouldn't you agree, Mic?" said Midnight, setting her sights on Mic's mouth.

"Thanks but no thanks! I make a point of not drinking stuff that looks like dirty dishwater!"

"Enough bellyaching... Just drink."

"No, wait... Stop!"

With adroit timing, Midnight poured the brownish-gray solution into Mic's open mouth.

"Well? Describe it. I need to know," she said, cheeks

flushed with a rush of blood and eyes glinting like a bird of prey's.

"Blech…"

Present Mic slumped down in his seat, and All Might trembled in fear.

A taste capable of shutting up Mic…? Terrifying… How lucky for me that I can't drink!

"Too stimulating for him, I suppose? Well, for my next creation, how about this…some of this, and… Hey, Chief? Can I borrow some condiments? Whatever you've got back there!"

"Never seen anything so irrational…" spat Aizawa between sips of beer, still going strong. Beside him, Mic came back to life.

"Gahh! That gutter water sent me straight to hell and back! My dearly deceased ancestors were coming in for a hug and about to gimme a tour of the place! Yikes!"

"In that case, this next one will have plenty of miso— the heart and soul of Japan and its people—and just the thing to please your ancestors… Heh, I wonder how it'll taste?" said Midnight. This got Thirteen's attention.

"Misho? That glorioush, miraculoush fermented gift from the earth! Raishing thoshe plantsh takesh fertile

shoil, which you get from the volcanoesh going BOOM and lotsh of rainwater shprinkling the fieldsh... Are you even lishening, Midnight?"

"Coming in loud and clear, Thirteen. Give me a second, and I'll have this miracle of nature ready for you," said Midnight.

"Abort mission, Thirteen! The only miracle would be you surviving a close encounter with that drink!" warned Mic.

"How rude. I'll try it first... Hmm... Intense, somehow nostalgic... Kind of bittersweet. Reminds me of a one-night stand."

"Whoa! How'd you turn that into a flavor?"

UA

All Might sat back and observed his colleagues letting their hair down—a side of them he'd never seen. Even as they squabbled and schemed, he was glad to see them generally having a good time. Still, he felt uncomfortable being the only one whose drinks weren't working quite the same magic.

I wonder if my being sober is somehow throwing a wet blanket on this party...

Maybe this group was usually even more animated? The more All Might thought about it, the guiltier he felt. Casting a glance at Midnight menacing the others with her deadly cocktails, All Might whispered to the silent Aizawa.

"I think I'll head out soon. But you guys have fun, okay?"

As he grabbed his bag and started to get up, All Might felt a hand grab his own. Aizawa released his grip just as quickly and started scratching his head, as if the sheepish hand didn't know what to do with itself. His listless eyes darted side to side a bit.

"What is it, Aizawa?"

"Why not stay a little longer?"

"Ah, but..."

"I wanted to tell you something today," muttered Aizawa, dropping his gaze.

"W-what?" asked All Might, steeling himself to get scolded by the teacher again for his deficiencies as an educator. He couldn't have been more off the mark.

"Thank you."

"Huh?"

"Because you fought for us all in Kamino...I didn't lose any students. They're still around for me to watch out for."

"Oh. That..." said All Might, feeling warmth well up in his chest. He'd spent his life fighting to keep people smiling, and here was visceral proof that his efforts had meant something.

"That's why...I'm thanking you."

I appreciate the sentiment more than you know, but alas...

"Aizawa, that's a daruma."

The whole time, Aizawa had been addressing the round, red daruma decorating the alcove just behind All Might.

"Knock it off, All Might. I'm being serious..."

"Me too! I'm telling you, you're talking to a daruma doll!"

"Whew! Eraser's good and drunk, looks like!" said Present Mic, who'd noticed Aizawa's mistake.

"Huh? Aizawa is actually drunk?" asked a shocked All Might.

"Since way earlier, yeah! Those finishing moves he used on me are proof! Also, he's the type who doesn't remember a thing about being drunk later on!"

All Might recalled Aizawa's earlier line about not remembering ever getting drunk.

How long do these parties usually run, I wonder?

Since Aizawa had stopped him, All Might couldn't very well leave early, and his lack of experience with such functions meant that he wasn't sure of the proper way to bring them to a close. As All Might pondered his dilemma, Thirteen blurted "Oh, I know!" and started to make a phone call.

"Ah. Cementossh? What do you think about the shplendor of nature? Wanna come chat with me and All Might about it?"

"Huh? Why Cementoss?" said All Might in surprise.

"Ah, another drunken habit of our young friend. He calls up anyone and everyone, hoping for conversation," explained Midnight.

"Hmm? Where're we drinking at? Shanzaru, of course. Ahem, Sanzaru."

UA

Not long after Thirteen made his call, the group was joined by Ectoplasm, Vlad King, Cementoss, and Hound Dog.

"Why did nobody inform me about this get-together earlier?" said Ectoplasm.

"We were just talking about drinking together sometime. This is perfect," said Vlad King.

"And now the gang's all here," said Cementoss.

"Wouldn't want the kids seeing us here like this... Grr..." growled Hound Dog.

Nine teachers now sat around the table, with Cementoss next to Thirteen, then Vlad King and Hound Dog. Ectoplasm joined Midnight on the other side. Each ordered drinks and food, leading to yet another toast.

Ah, we could be here awhile, now! thought All Might, hiding his frustration with a forced smile.

Hound Dog lapped up a few sips of his sake and spoke.

"Everything in moderation, okay? We're supposed to be setting examples for the kids."

And that's why Hound Dog is fit to be school life supervisor!

All Might nodded vigorously in agreement, feeling reassured that the strict, by-the-books Hound Dog would keep this party from getting out of control. Once again, though, he couldn't have been more wrong.

"I've never felt prouder to be class B's homeroom teacher!" shouted Vlad King passionately, slamming his fists on the table. He was already on his third whiskey-and-soda highball.

"Didn't expect any less from the parents of my brave little go-getters, but still... When they agreed to put their children's safety in my hands, it...it...made my heart leap!"

A deluge of sloppy tears drip-dropped into Vlad's mug.

"One highball, extra salt?" quipped Midnight.

So Vlad King is a weepy drunk, apparently...

Seeing the grown man cry knocked All Might off-balance a little, but he recovered and said, "The class A parents were good sports about it too, right, Aizawa?"

"Mhm," said Aizawa with a nod.

"Class A too, huh... A toast to both our classes, Eraser!" said Vlad, still openly crying. On his knees, he

shuffled over toward Aizawa with mug in hand, forced his colleague to clink, and drained his salty highball.

"I admit your kids have taken a tiny lead so far...but class B is gonna catch up soon, and then some. Cuz my kids've got talent and drive to spare!" said Vlad.

Aizawa bristled. "Yeah. Well. So do mine."

Vlad froze, and the tears dried up.

"I recognize class A's superiority, for now. But my kids' talents make them better suited to open-minded teamwork! Meanwhile, all those standout Quirks in your class make it harder for yours to work together, since they're each trying to hog the spotlight!"

Aizawa scowled at Vlad's obvious provocation.

"You act like teamwork is the end-all, be-all. Of course it matters, but first they need to figure out their Quirks and train to use them individually."

"That's a vase, Aizawa," said All Might, who'd been observing the war of words between homeroom teachers. As it happened, Aizawa's argument had been directed at a decorative vase just next to the daruma he had mistaken for All Might.

"Did you say something, All Might?"

"Yes, but now you're talking to the daruma again."

"Fool! Class B's got the best kids! They're my precious little scamps!" said an increasingly emotional Vlad. Without waiting for another response from Aizawa, he started weeping again. Next to them, Midnight gulped down another of her mystery cocktails with a smug look of satisfaction.

"Let's go to karaoke, everyone. We can keep drinking and sing while we're at it," suggested Ectoplasm, but the others were too caught up in their own nonsense to hear him. Thirteen suddenly remembered something and draped himself over All Might.

"All Might, let'sh continue our talk about the importansh of water," he said, still slurring his words.

"Huh? Right! Very important, water! No doubt!"

"Sho how do we really protect thish planet'sh water, then? Gimme your thoughtsh!"

All Might felt pinned between a space suit and a hard place, but a neighbor was ready with aid.

"Knock it off, Thirteen. You're bothering All Might… I can handle him, All Might. Don't you worry," said Cementoss with a warm smile. Thirteen took this as an invitation and sidled up to his bulky colleague.

"What do you think about water, Cementossh?" said Thirteen.

"I think it's a great gift from Mother Nature herself. How about you, Thirteen?"

"Agreed! A precioush gift from nature!"

All Might was impressed with Cementoss's skillful pivot, but then he noticed Thirteen's space suit helmet in Cementoss's hands. The man was stroking the helmet gently, as if pacifying a small animal. Though Present Mic had been mocking Aizawa's drunken state, he now noticed All Might's confusion and explained.

"That's just how Cementoss gets when he's drunk! The guy loves round things, I guess. Weird fetish, huh!"

"Care to give something round of mine a good rub?" teased Midnight.

"That's inappropriate," said Cementoss, with his characteristic flat smile.

"Would anyone else like to go to karaoke? It would be fun, I'm sure," said Ectoplasm, but once again he was drowned out by the others' banter. After a few more failed attempts, he got fed up and stood. That got their attention.

"Enough! I will go to karaoke alone!" said Ectoplasm

before falling over backward. Midnight caught him before he could hit the floor and laid his head on her lap.

"Is he okay?" asked All Might in a worried voice.

"Just his bedtime, that's all," said Midnight. Indeed, Ectoplasm was out like a light and snoring loudly.

"Nature's own memory foam pillow! Color me jealous!" yelped Mic.

All Might suddenly felt exhausted.

They're only getting more and more wasted... Why, Hound Dog is the only one left with his senses about him!

Hoping to confirm his own thoughts, All Might turned toward Hound Dog at the end of the table.

"One bone... Two bones... Three bones... Hee hee."

At some point, Hound Dog had collected everyone's bone-shaped chopstick rests, which he now stared at while lapping up sake.

Spoke too soon.

It made perfect sense, since Hound Dog's Quirk gave him canine features and qualities. Vlad King stopped weeping and bragging about class B long enough to notice the bones, too.

"Collecting bones there, Hound Dog...? Pass your bones this way, gang! We got a dog in need!" said Vlad,

still crying. It seemed like anything could set the man off when he had alcohol in him. Once all the chopstick rests were piled in front of Hound Dog, the canine hero's eyes started getting misty.

"Thank you."

"Don't mention it, pal... A toast! To your bones!" said Vlad. The two friends clinked to commemorate the moment.

"Youth is a beautiful thing," said Midnight, stroking the sleeping Ectoplasm's hair and taking a swig of one of her cocktails. At that moment, Ectoplasm's eyes popped open. He sprang to his feet, gripped an empty beer bottle like a microphone, and started singing to an unheard melody.

"E-Ectoplasm?" said a stunned All Might. Across the table, Mic took a beer bottle for himself and started emceeing.

"Attention, villains throughout the land... There's a hero standing up to fight back... Yeah, Ectoplasm's got a song for this cruel, harsh world... It's that old, classic hit 'Heroes' Bar,' so don't touch that dial!"

With Mic's intro over, Ectoplasm's refined, dulcet tones started in right on cue.

"Besting villains takes a toll, and heroes need some sustenance…"

"An oldie but goodie!"

"Your costume's stench may sting the eyes."

"Sure, cuz who's got time for laundry?"

"But come as you are, to the heroes' bar!"

"Bar! Hey, that's where we are!"

"Serving up smiles, for one and all!"

"You've got a great smile too, pal."

As though in a trance, Ectoplasm went through the song. Mic made his quips between the lyrics. The whole table cheered. Just another staple of drinking parties, it seemed.

How do I get out of here…?

All Might was feeling at a loss when Ectoplasm dove right into a second interminable song. As the party's single sober participant, he felt like the only one with the power to end it. Unfortunately, he hadn't a clue how to go about it amid the noise and chaos. He slipped

away to the restroom to clear his head, but even that couldn't snap him out of his funk. On the way back to the table, All Might bumped into Mic in the corridor.

"Heyyy, All Might. You look bushed!"

"Ha ha ha… Just surprised that you guys always manage to party this hard," said All Might with a weak, forced laugh.

"Always?" said Mic, looking puzzled.

"Huh? It's not always like this, then?"

"Nah, today's special. Our usual teetotalers are drinking, and our boozehounds are really knocking them back."

"What's special about today…?" It was All Might's turn to look puzzled.

"It ain't every day we get a chance to drink with the greatest hero around. You're the hero the heroes look up to, man," said Mic with a grin. "Whoops, my bladder's about to burst! Scuse me!" he added before rushing to the restroom.

From the corridor, All Might surveyed the other seven at the table. The scene had resembled some chaotic layer of hell just a moment ago, but Mic's words had put things in a new light. The final lyric of "Heroes' Bar" sprang into his mind.

"'Serving up smiles,' was it…? Heh," said All Might, chuckling to himself.

His nonalcoholic beer didn't have to spoil the fun. Not when he had his new colleagues' smiles to keep him going. He found this resolve just in time, because the party suddenly noticed his absence.

"Where'sh All Might gone to?" asked Thirteen.

"He's right here, you," said Aizawa.

"Eraser, that's the daruma again."

"Huh? Did he just up and go home?"

All Might smiled and called out to the panicking table as he walked back. "Just a trip to the bathroom, that's all."

At once, the entire group (minus Aizawa) stood up and crowded around him.

"We shtill haven't chatted about nature! Oh, I know! Let'sh go shee those Yakushima cedarsh right now and talk about 'em until dawn!" said Thirteen.

"But the planes and trains have already stopped for the night!" protested All Might.

"Why don't I whip up a cocktail that'll give you the full Yakushima experience, then?" said Midnight.

"Cedar flavored? No thanks! That's bound to be one bitter drink!" said All Might.

"All Might, if you need to relax, why not try rubbing this delightfully round helmet? I find it helps me clear my mind. Oh, but then I'll need something else that's round for myself... No matter. Lend me those biceps of yours, Vlad?" said Cementoss.

"Now you're the one being inappropriate, Cementoss."

"Maybe I can go without that sweet, sweet roundness for a minute..." conceded Cementoss.

"Never mind that. Let's go to karaoke. They have special discounts at this hour," said Ectoplasm.

"Ooh! A chance to hear All Might himself belt one out...? I'm getting emotional just thinking about it! Eh, Hound Dog?" said Vlad.

"Ah... Ah... Awooo!"

"That's Hound Dog's happy howl, for sure."

"I'm really not much of a singer..." protested All Might.

"But All Might is over here..." said Aizawa, who hadn't glommed on to All Might with the others. He reached clumsily for the daruma on the shelf, sending it rolling to the floor.

"Are you hurt, All Might...?"

"For the last time, Aizawa, that's a daruma!"

Still yammering away, the clingy group of drunks brought All Might back to the table in the tatami corner.

"Why don't we take it easy, everyone?" said All Might, but there was no reasoning with them anymore. The happy thought of being served up smiles evaporated, and All Might swore to himself that this would be his final drinking party.

UA

Sanzaru was a small izakaya tucked away in a back alley near U.A. High, and its name referenced the three wise monkeys who see, hear, and speak no evil. Despite the noble origins of the imagery, a humbler, more straightforward interpretation was perhaps warranted here—what happens in the izakaya stays in the izakaya. In that sense, heroes and educators alike could spend a night drinking and unwinding without the usual pomp and circumstance. They too were only human, after all.

Part 2
Dramatic Makeover!

WHAT COULD THE ALWAYS-COOL TODOROKI'S ROOM BE LIKE...? I'M ON PINS AND NEEDLES...

OUR CLASS'S BEST-LOOKING GUY.

OUR CLASS'S MOST CAPABLE STUDENT.

In one wing of the Yaoyorozu family's palatial mansion, a pile of several dozen cardboard boxes stacked like a pyramid seemed out of place within Momo Yaoyorozu's elegantly decorated room. Yaoyorozu sighed, relieved to be done with her packing at last.

"Momo?" said her mother, entering the room. In her shadow was the family butler, Uchimura.

"Well? Are you prepared for your big move?"

"I've just finished packing, Mother. I tried to make everything as compact as possible, yet..." Yaoyorozu furrowed her brow in discontent.

Her mother wore a look of concern as well, but for a different reason. "Will you manage with so little? Did you pack a tea set large enough for your entire class, so that nobody feels left out at teatime? And how about your evening dresses?"

Her mother's particular concerns did nothing to ease Yaoyorozu's expression.

"Surely those things aren't necessary, Mother..."

She would never need to wear a dress to class, and a tea set with service for eight was plenty. Besides, Yaoyorozu assumed that her classmates would each be bringing their own personal cups, saucers, and sugar bowls.

"It never hurts to be prepared, Momo," said Mrs. Yaoyorozu flatly, which made her daughter start to doubt herself.

"No, I suppose you're right. What if we were to have a party in class one day..." said Yaoyorozu.

"Uchimura?"

A word and a glance from the lady of the house prompted a small nod from the butler; he understood his employer's wishes without a full explanation.

"Another cardboard box, ma'am? Of course. I've also been informed by U.A. that a maid may not accompany Miss Momo within the dormitory, so I've taken the liberty of purchasing the latest models of household appliances," said Uchimura.

"All of which are sure to be useful for the other students as well! Wonderful! Ah, and we mustn't forget entertainment—the contents of the playroom will have to be packed as well."

"Please understand… The school dormitory will be a place of education and training. We're meant to be as self-sufficient as possible," said Yaoyorozu, objecting to her mother's frivolous additions to the packing list.

"Miss Momo, are you quite sure…?"

"Oh, Momo…"

Tears welled up in her mother's eyes.

"Forgive me. I just never expected you to be leaving the nest this soon, so I can't help but worry."

"How impertinent of me to presume to advise," lamented the butler, hanging his head.

"Mother… Uchimura…" said Yaoyorozu, feeling the love and running up to them. "I'm sorry, but thank you for understanding! And the sentiment is very much appreciated!"

"You'll be all grown up soon, Momo… But yes, of course. If you take nothing else, at least accept this gift, purchased to commemorate your new life in the dormitory. Uchimura?"

"Ahem," said Uchimura, signaling the maids in the hallway to wheel in a handcart with about ten more cardboard boxes. Yaoyorozu opened one and found it was nearly bursting at the seams with new books.

"An encyclopedia set with reference books from every country of the world, Miss Momo. Your father was sure this would please you more than anything. You will also find custom-made bookshelves," explained Uchimura.

"Oh! Of course I'll have to bring these with me!" said Yaoyorozu, nearly moved to tears. Mrs. Yaoyorozu and Uchimura watched her warmly, feeling a bit more emotionally prepared for the girl they cared for to leave home.

UA

It was a clear mid-August day, and the students of class 1-A stood, reunited, before their brand-new Heights Alliance dorm building.

Aizawa had just informed the class that Shoto Todoroki, Eijiro Kirishima, Izuku Midoriya, Yaoyorozu, and Tenya Ida had set out to rescue the kidnapped

Katsuki Bakugo. Though their teacher's unforgiving reprimand darkened the mood for a moment, Bakugo's particular brand of blunt gratitude pepped everyone up a bit before they headed inside the building.

With five floors and a basement, each dormitory building would be home to one class. The first floor featured the dining area, the baths, a laundry room, and a common area equipped with a TV and sofas.

Aizawa had already assigned the students to specific bedrooms on floors two through five. Minoru Mineta, Midoriya, Yuga Aoyama, and Fumikage Tokoyami would be living on the second floor. Wary of Mineta's presence, Aizawa hadn't put any girls on that floor.

The third floor would house Koji Koda, Denki Kaminari, Ida, Mashirao Ojiro, Kyoka Jiro, and Toru Hagakure. Then, Mezo Shoji, Kirishima, Bakugo, Ochaco Uraraka, and Mina Ashido on the fourth, and Rikido Sato, Todoroki, Hanta Sero, Yaoyorozu, and Tsuyu Asui on the fifth.

The building itself and everything inside still had that brand-new look and smell, which only made the kids more excited for this radical change in their lives.

"Today's set aside for settling in," said Aizawa to the

group. "We'll talk about what comes next tomorrow. Dismissed!"

"Yes, Sensei!" said the students in unison, with genuine energy. While most moved toward the elevators and the upper floors, Aizawa called Yaoyorozu aside.

"Not all of your things will fit," he said, gesturing at the pyramid of boxes that now sat in a corner of the first-floor common area. The stack was even taller than before because of the additional encyclopedia set and bookshelves.

"You'll have to pick just five or six boxes to keep. Only the bare essentials. Send the rest back."

"Five or six?" stammered Yaoyorozu. "Surely you jest, Sensei!"

UA

While Yaoyorozu was agonizing over how best to pare down her possessions, Todoroki was dumbstruck by what he'd discovered when he'd opened the door to his new room on the fifth floor.

No tatami mats.

He shouldn't have been surprised; he'd just seen the synthetic flooring in some of his classmates' rooms in passing, but since Todoroki had only ever known his family's traditional Japanese home, a part of his brain had expected his dorm room to follow suit.

The kids were allowed to use the bed, desk, and dresser set furnished by the school or to bring their own furniture, so Todoroki was now looking at the *wadansu* dresser, *fuzukue* desk, low *zaisu* chair, and futon straight from his room at home, as well as a cardboard box containing his clothes and other small necessities.

He scowled in spite of himself, perhaps because of the stark disconnect between his traditional furniture and the sleek, modern flooring. Some interior designers might be able to work some feng shui to successfully blend Eastern and Western aesthetics, but no such artist had paid this room a visit.

Todoroki's gaze settled on the window next, and he noticed the curtains provided by the school.

No shoji window panels either...

Still feeling like something was off, he walked to the window and absentmindedly opened and shut the curtains. He was used to the curtains at school, but never in a room where he slept.

Why am I so rattled? Just because of these strips of cloth…?

After all, in the end, wasn't his near and dear shoji paneling just strips of paper attached to wooden frames? In any case, there was no obvious way to convert this room into a traditional Japanese one, so Todoroki tried to take his mind off the matter. Before setting out to unpack his things, he changed into a light, breathable top and took off his socks—a habit from back at home, where tatami mats covered the floor. No sooner had he done so, though, than he became acutely aware of his feet sticking and slapping against the synthetic flooring. This didn't do anything to help his mood, but he shook off the odd sensation and starting transferring his clothes from the box into the dresser.

The box contained clothes, a towel, and a photo album. Todoroki's older sister, Fuyumi, had also tossed in some small decorations—including a bonsai tree—so that his dorm room wouldn't look too bleak. Since he only had the one box, the move-in job was over quickly. With nothing else to do, Todoroki flopped

onto the floor in the middle of the room and stared at the white, round light fixture on the ceiling. Then, another realization.

No pull cord for the light… I have to walk over to the door to flip the switch?

The Todoroki family house had square, wooden fixtures that hung low from the ceiling. When it was time for bed, one needed only to tug the string dangling a few feet above one's futon. Here, the dorm room's light switch was by the door. Turning off the light would only take a few seconds, but the unfamiliarity of it irked Todoroki.

He surveyed the room, noting the ceiling and white walls lacking Japanese-style wooden struts. Then, his traditional furniture. The slick flooring. Still on his back, Todoroki rolled his head side to side to get a feel for the floor's texture; unlike his beloved tatami mats, it was unforgivingly hard.

So this is where I'll be sleeping from now on.

He thought he'd understood what it meant to move out of the house, but now he could feel it with his entire body. There'd been days in his life when Todoroki wanted nothing more than a way to stop sleeping under a roof provided by the father he hated. He hadn't expected that day would come so soon, though.

Endeavor had grumbled when he'd learned about the implementation of the dorm system, but he'd still agreed to let Todoroki go. All Might's sudden retirement meant that Endeavor could no longer achieve his lifelong goal of surpassing the active number one hero, so he'd been in no mood to argue about smaller matters.

That bastard went to U.A. too, didn't he...?

Todoroki couldn't help but wonder what sort of student his father had been back in high school, but he quickly shook his head in an attempt to rid himself of the intrusive thoughts. The back of his head bumped against the hard floor again, making him spring up in irritation. Hoping to clear his mind, he walked to the window, opened it, and took a deep breath of fresh air.

The forest beyond the window seemed to go on forever, punctuated only by the various facilities of U.A. dotting the landscape here and there. The U.A. grounds were almost frighteningly large, but even this grand view from the top floor of Heights Alliance couldn't snap Todoroki out of his funk. He retrieved

his photo album from a drawer, gently removed a single photo, and walked out onto the veranda.

The colors in his photo were a bit faded, but Todoroki could still clearly make out the image of himself as a child, held by his mother. This was before she had burned him, of course, and the photo showed her smiling. Happy, even. Todoroki had once hated photos like this one, since they only reminded him that his mother would probably never smile like that again. It was different now, though, since he'd already been proven wrong.

Just as Todoroki's bad mood started to fade and his expression began to soften, a strong gust of wind snatched the photo from his hands and sent it flying. He dashed out of Heights Alliance in a panic.

It must've landed somewhere around here...

Todoroki frantically scanned the forest floor, but given the size of the grounds, his lost photo might as well have been a needle in a haystack. He followed the paths leading to the scattered facilities but came up with nothing.

Where'd it go…?

Suddenly, he heard a metallic clanging from off in the distance. A fist-sized device came zooming at Todoroki, so he tossed up a quick ice wall to defend himself. The object smacked into the ice and fell to the ground.

"What the hell?"

"Ah, my sweet baby!"

The voice came from Support Course student Mei Hatsume, who burst out of the trees in her trademark tank top and massive goggle headgear. It took him a second, but Todoroki recognized her as a fellow competitor from the Sports Festival and handed her the small machine.

"Thanks! This little one's my forty-eighth precious baby. Perfect if you need to capture a villain and— Oh no, my baby!"

Hatsume gasped as what must have been another one of her machines flew by. Some also rumbled and rolled over the ground in the surrounding forest.

"Wait up, baby!" she cried, running after the device.

"There're some over there, too," said Todoroki, who,

putting two and two together, realized that what Hatsume called "babies" were actually just her inventions.

"Round them up for me, would you?"

"Huh? For real?"

Hatsume ignored Todoroki's protest and ran out of sight. It took him a moment to process the situation. Sure, the machines clearly mattered to her, but he was out here looking for something important too. Another gust of wind disturbed the branches of nearby trees. Getting caught up in Hatsume's business just meant giving the photo more time to get blown to who knows where.

Still, he placed a wall of ice in the path of one incoming machine, stopping it in its tracks. There— he'd contributed. Todoroki ran off in search of his photo again, but he could still hear the clanging coming from somewhere in the forest. Many of Hatsume's machines were roving about the woods, and Todoroki started to doubt himself.

He recalled his classmate Ida. When Todoroki and the others had set out to rescue Bakugo on their own, the straitlaced Ida had opposed the decision vehemently enough to lose his usual composure. He was dead set against the group of students possibly getting caught up in a battle, so in the end, he had agreed to join the rescue effort as a sort of monitor. Ida's older brother had nearly been murdered by the Hero Killer, Stain, but even if that history hadn't driven his decision, the class president's serious nature was bolstered by a heavy sense of duty and responsibility.

What would Ida do, here...?

Todoroki stopped and spun around, because the answer was obvious—Ida would help a person in need without a moment's hesitation. As would anyone hoping to become a hero.

The photo still weighed on his mind, but Todoroki followed the sounds and got to work with his ice walls.

Meanwhile, in a room on the third floor of Heights Alliance, Ida was pondering how best to organize his many books.

"Alphabetically, by author's last name? Or perhaps by topic...? Or by publisher? Should I take the number of times I've read each book into consideration? Or I could simply arrange them by size... But what about..."

Ida gasped.

"I could very well angst about this all day, and there'd be no end to it! As class president, I ought to help the others get their rooms sorted! In the meantime, my books will be just fine arranged by spine color!"

He began to place his books on shelves with unusual efficiency. Yes, dorm life would suit the class president just fine.

UA

"Thanks for helping me round up my supercute babies!" said Hatsume.

After collecting the nearby machines, Todoroki and Hatsume had met back up and introduced themselves. It turned out that while moving in, Hatsume had been transporting her support-item inventions when an accident had somehow flipped the machines' on switches, causing them to run amok.

"You mean you made all of these? Wow."

There were enough machines to fill an entire cart, which she'd been pulling along when the accident occurred.

"Heh. All my love and talent goes into these babies! Oh, this one happens to be my pride and joy!" said Hatsume, reaching into the mountain of machines with both arms. She pulled out a device on wheels, about as big as one of the cardboard boxes for moving day.

"Just push this button here, and..."

The device whirred and clanked as it grew into a miniature mobile crane.

"It might look compact, but I made this baby to capture gigantic villains. See the tip of the long boom? It shoots out wires that even the rowdiest villain couldn't shake loose from. Heh heh, awesome, right? Oh, or how about this gauntlet? It's a baby that'll multiply your grip strength ten times over and let you go toe-to-toe with muscle-bound villains, even! And then there's this one, which..."

Hatsume's love for each and every one of her dear inventions was on full display. Todoroki listened patiently to her lengthy, exuberant explanations and only spoke up once she was finished.

"So. Is that all of them?"

"Lemme see..." said Hatsume, surveying the pile. Her eyebrows twitched. "Still missing one."

"What's it look like?"

"It's a teeny-tiny baby, but way heavier than you'd think. My thought was, you can somehow attach it to a villain so they can't make a run for it so easily!"

"How small are we talking?"

"About as big as a cherry? If fruit's your thing."

"A cherry, huh..." said Todoroki as he scanned the area. "Something that heavy couldn't have rolled too far, right?"

"True! I'll use my Quirk to look for it, since my eyes can zoom in from up to five kilometers away!"

"Sure. And I'll check behind the trees and wherever else you can't see."

They began to search, but before peeking behind too many trees, Todoroki remembered his own predicament.

"Oh. If you spot a photograph on the ground, let me know."

"A photo? Sure thing! Is that what you were out here looking for in the first place?"

"Yeah..."

"My, my, what are you two kids doing out and about? I thought today was the big move-in day."

The third voice came from Youthful Hero: Recovery Girl, whose efforts to stay fit led her to take brisk walks around the school grounds. Hatsume explained the situation to the aged school nurse.

"I would be happy to help you look," said Recovery Girl, who joined the hunt and began checking behind trees with Todoroki.

"Not over here... Ack!" cried Recovery Girl, tripping over a tree root. Todoroki lunged to catch her, but she kept herself upright with some quick footwork. Todoroki's rescue attempt earned him a smile from Recovery Girl.

"Ready to save me, were you? Thank you, but I've got more pep in my step than that, yet."

She stared a bit harder at Todoroki.

"It still hasn't hit me that Endeavor's boy is so grown up already."

"Huh...?"

"I've been at U.A. a long time, you know? Known your father since he was a student here."

This mention of his father darkened Todoroki's face, as if by reflex.

"I was always treating him for scrapes, cuts, and bruises back in those days. That boy put himself through the wringer, hoping to be the number one hero someday."

Recovery Girl's reminiscence triggered Todoroki's memories from childhood and beyond—the sound of his father's voice shouting at him. The voice always commanded the boy to succeed where his father had failed and grow into a hero who could surpass All Might. Todoroki hated that voice with a passion.

"Why, your father was so driven that, one time, in class..."

"I'd rather not hear anything about that bastard... ma'am," interrupted Todoroki.

Recovery Girl's face softened, and she gave the boy an apologetic smile.

"Yes, of course, I'm sorry. Nobody picks their family, I suppose."

Todoroki felt himself growing gloomier by the minute. It wouldn't be until the upcoming provisional license exam that he'd face head-on his own frustration and inability to process these feelings about his father.

A loud beeping—almost like a warning signal—sounded from the road beyond the trees, followed by Hatsume's voice saying, "Hang on, that's weird!"

"Now what could that be?" said Recovery Girl, trotting off toward the source of the noise.

Still grappling with his thoughts, Todoroki watched the school nurse walk away and decided to keep searching among the trees. Behind one large tree, his foot snagged on something and he pitched forward. He was sure it was another root, but he turned to find that he'd tripped over a round object the size of a large cherry. He tried to pick it up, but it wouldn't budge. This had to be Hatsume's deceptively heavy support item.

"Hey, I found it—" said Todoroki, but his voice was drowned out by more of that destructive, mechanical clanging. He raced over to find the mini mobile crane poised to capture Recovery Girl. Nearby, Hatsume frantically mashed buttons on a remote control, clearly attempting to stop her runaway creation.

"What's going on now?" said Todoroki.

"It fired up on its own! The circuitry must've gotten damaged when it fell outta the cart! I think it's convinced that Recovery Girl's a villain who needs to be hog-tied!" explained Hatsume.

"Eek!" cried Recovery Girl as she turned to flee. She tripped over her own feet, though, and the crane seized the opportunity to launch binding wires from the tip of its boom. Todoroki leaped toward Recovery Girl with timing that couldn't have been worse; the crane's wires wrapped around them both.

"Good effort, but…" said Recovery Girl.

"Sorry, ma'am."

As Todoroki apologized for his bungled rescue attempt, he couldn't help but think of another classmate, Kirishima. The two boys hadn't spoken much before the team-up to save Bakugo, but Kirishima's reluctance to sit idly by while the villains held his kidnapped friend had inspired Todoroki to take action at the time. He'd understood how Kirishima felt, of course, given that Todoroki had witnessed firsthand when the villains had snatched the compressed orb holding Bakugo during the attack on their training camp. It was why Todoroki had agreed to join the rescue effort, so now he found himself reflecting on his classmate's passion and courage in the face of trouble.

It's times like these when Kirishima lets his gut decide for him.

UA

At that moment, Kirishima was helping his new neighbor Bakugo unpack his things on the fourth floor of Heights Alliance. One of Bakugo's boxes had somehow found its way into Kirishima's room, and when the latter had returned it, one thing had led to another.

"Yo, Bakugo! What's this stick thing? Some sorta weapon?"

"A walking stick, for mountain climbing... Hey, who said you could stick around? Don'tchu got your own crap to unpack?"

Kirishima returned Bakugo's grimace with a goofy grin.

"Don't they say two heads are better that one? But don't worry—you can help me with my room after this!"

"Like hell I will! It's quicker doing this stuff alone."

Despite Bakugo's harsh words, he made no extra effort to kick Kirishima out.

A savior, and the one who'd been saved; if there'd been any lingering awkwardness over recent events, the breeze blowing through the window of the new dorm room cleared it away, just like that.

U.A.

Todoroki squirmed, trying to shake off the wires, but he and Recovery Girl were bound fast, with arms strapped down against their bodies. Each jerk only made the strong metal wires squeeze around them tighter.

"It's gonna pinch even harder if you move around!" shouted Hatsume. "So just stay still!"

"Get this crap off of us," said Todoroki.

"Would if I could, but the remote control's on the fritz too!"

Shoot... What would Yaoyorozu do in this situation?

Like Ida, Yaoyorozu had voiced her opposition to the Bakugo rescue operation, but she'd decided to accompany the boys just in case they'd needed to be reined in. She never failed to see the big picture, and Todoroki knew that if Yaoyorozu were in his shoes, she would keep a level head and use her impressive brainpower to come up with a clever plan.

UA

Yaoyorozu was still on the first floor, deciding which of her possessions sparked joy and which she could do without.

"My silverware made of pure silver... Unnecessary. And I only need a single painting to hang. As for shoes... Three pairs should be enough... Ah, I ought to keep a pair of high heels, just in case... But where would I store them...? No, only the bare essentials... Right. Just one pair of shoes, then!"

Though Todoroki was none the wiser, Yaoyorozu was making full use of that quick decision-making he admired.

UA

Todoroki plunged into thought.

He could probably freeze the wires or even burn them away with his Quirk, but either option was bound to hurt Recovery Girl, given that they were tied to each other.

"It's a real shame, but I'm gonna have to tear my baby apart piece by piece at this rate... Just need to run and grab my tools from the studio!" said Hatsume. But just as she turned to leave, the mini crane began to drive forward with Todoroki and Recovery Girl still dangling from the boom. It picked up speed as it moved down the road leading to one of U.A.'s facilities.

"W-what's going on?" said Recovery Girl.

"Not so fast, my baby!"

With a twinkle in her eye, Hatsume equipped her power gauntlet and grabbed the crane from behind. It showed no sign of slowing, though, and even began dragging her.

"Careful! That's not gonna work!" said Todoroki.

"Hurry and fetch a teacher, now!" said Recovery Girl.

That was when Todoroki laid eyes on something troubling ahead.

"What's a giant pit doing out here?"

"The second-years were using it for training. They say it goes down pretty deep..." said Recovery Girl with a grim expression. It was true; even hoisted up in the air by the crane, they couldn't see the bottom of the pit. Falling in while attached to the runaway machine would be disastrous, and Todoroki had a hard time hiding his panic.

The crane picked up speed again, making a beeline

for the pit. No time for Hatsume to run and get help. Todoroki knew he could use his Quirk as a last resort, but that came with its own issues.

What can I do...?

The face of another classmate arose in Todoroki's mind.

Obviously Midoriya would never just give up...

During the mission to rescue Bakugo, the kids had found themselves a stone's throw from the grand battle between All Might and the villainous All For One, but even when all hope had seemed lost, Midoriya had come up with a plan to fly across the battlefield and get the job done. This would be the same friend who'd help Todoroki come to terms with the hatred for his father that was holding him back.

[A]

Midoriya was grappling with his own problem in his new room on the second floor.

"Silver Age, Golden Age, suited version? Is that a good order...? Ah, but I'd hate to leave out the in-flight version..."

Beyond daily necessities and weight training equipment, the lion's share of Midoriya's personal effects were All Might collectibles. He'd already hung his All Might posters on the wall and stuck his All Might books on the shelves, next to his textbooks.

"But sometimes the *chibi* figure is just what I need to feel right at home! And the one in a flexing pose inspires me when I'm feeling down... Hmm!"

Moderation was not a word in Midoriya's vocabulary when it came to merchandise related to his personal idol. Everything had to be arranged in just the right spots, in the right order, at the right angles. Until his room was decorated to perfection, Midoriya wouldn't give up.

UA

As his thoughts turned to his friend for inspiration, perhaps it was better that Todoroki didn't know exactly what Midoriya was up to in that moment. Then, it came to him. He swung around toward Hatsume—who was rummaging through her pile of machines looking for a solution—and shouted.

"Get your heavy cherry and toss it at me!"

"Huh?"

"Quickly! It's behind that biggest tree, right over there!"

"No clue what you're thinking, but sure, fine!" said Hatsume as she dove into the trees. She spotted the weighted ball without much trouble and picked it up with her gauntlet. With the aid of some leg-enhancing armor, she dashed back to the crane at full speed.

"I've got it! You really want me to toss it at you?"

"Yeah, aim right for my mouth!"

Without missing a beat, Hatsume activated her Quirk, "Zoom," and zeroed in on Todoroki's open mouth before pitching the cherry-sized weight with all her strength. Todoroki caught the ball in his mouth and used the momentum and new center of gravity to swing his body to the side. The mini mobile crane's wheels on the opposite side lifted off the ground, so for a moment, it was driving on only two of the four wheels. With the yawning pit already a bit too close for comfort, the crane began to topple.

What now…?

Straining to hold on to the weight between his jaws, Todoroki managed to spin himself and Recovery Girl around just before they hit the ground, so that he alone would break the fall. The crane crashed against the road at the very edge of the pit.

"Close call, you two! Anyone hurt?" said Hatsume as she ran over.

Todoroki shook his head, spat out the weighted ball, and said, "Nuh-uh."

"I'm just fine too," said Recovery Girl.

"Phew! But man, using my weighted baby to stop my other rampaging baby? Great thinking! Never imagined using it that way, myself. Heh heh, I'm already cooking up news plans for it!"

"That's nice," said Todoroki. "Mind doing something about these wires?"

"Sure, right—lemme grab those tools! Be right back!"

This time Hatsume did run straight to the studio at the school, returning with both her tools and her mentor, Power Loader. She clipped the wires, finally freeing Todoroki and Recovery Girl. Apparently, Hatsume had already gotten a talking-to from Power Loader.

"So sorry for the trouble!" came the quick, forced apology from Hatsume.

"Hatsume, I know I told you to clean out the studio, but

I didn't mean you should bring all those support items to your dorm room," said Power Loader, clearly exasperated.

"Where, then? I don't have anywhere else to put my babies," said Hatsume.

"Well, we'd really be in trouble if this happened again in the dorms, so... Fine. Leave them in the studio."

"Gee, thanks. Wish you'd agreed to that sooner, Sensei."

Even during a good scolding, Hatsume hardly seemed repentant.

"Oh, hang on!" she said, remembering something and reaching into her pocket. "Spotted this caught on a tree branch on my way back. Gotta be what you were looking for, yeah?"

A relieved smile rose on Todoroki's face as she handed him the photo of him and his mother.

"Yeah. Thanks."

"Thanks? I should be thanking you for rounding up all my precious babies, and I know just the way to do it properly," said Hatsume. She reached into the pile of machines and pulled out a familiar-looking toy barrel, about the size of a basketball. "Enjoy, heh heh. Give it a go with your friends, and lemme know what you all think."

With that, she and Power Loader headed back to the studio with the cart full of inventions.

"Well, that was quite an adventure we just had… What's this? You're hurt?" said Recovery Girl, noticing a scrape on Todoroki's cheek from when the crane had toppled over. A quick Quirk-powered kiss healed his injury, and Recovery Girl then offered him gummy candy from her pocket.

"They're Haribo bears, so eat up, now. You get extra for saving me back there."

"No problem. Really," said Todoroki, accepting the pile of candy with a blank look on his face. "I mean, any of my friends would've done the same."

He wondered when he'd begun thinking of them that way. As friends. He was a little shocked to realize that they were already such fixtures in his life that he'd found himself turning to them for inspiration in a crisis— something he'd never really done before. Todoroki recognized that this was the kind of growing he needed to do. He knew he was lucky to be attending U.A.

"Of course they would have," said Recovery Girl, noticing Todoroki's expression relax a little. "All the

boys and girls at U.A. tend to do their darndest. They always have. So be sure to give yourself credit where credit is due, now and then."

"Yes, ma'am."

Todoroki popped a gummy bear into his mouth. The chewy candy gave his tired body the small burst of sugar it needed.

Guess she's saying that my bastard of a father did his best when he was here, too...?

He shook his head side to side to drive off the fleeting thought.

"Anyhow, have you finished moving in yet? Excited about living with all your classmates?" asked Recovery Girl, reminding Todoroki how uncomfortable he'd been feeling in his new dorm room. He opened up to the school nurse, explaining his particular problem.

"Is that so? I may have just the answer, then," she said, before leading Todoroki to a warehouse on the school grounds.

"What is this place...?"

"It's where we store furniture and other bulky garbage before tossing it."

The massive building was full of things that the

school no longer had use for. Todoroki's eyes lit up when they came upon a collection of tatami mats, some shoji window panels, and a square, wooden light fixture sitting in one corner.

"These were once used for some class or another, but you're free to have them. I'll be sure to let Aizawa know," said Recovery Girl.

"Thank you for this," said Todoroki, bowing. He took a few deep breaths as he watched Recovery Girl walk off.

A new room for a new lifestyle. There were sure to be plenty of unfamiliar experiences ahead, but nothing a student of U.A. couldn't handle. Todoroki rolled up his sleeves, ready to get down to work.

Part 3
Playtime Is Over!

Toru Hagakure's scream echoed across the first floor of Heights Alliance.

"Ahh! Peeping Tom!"

"Hang on, isn't Mineta in the bath?" said Denki Kaminari, who came racing over from the common area with Mashirao Ojiro and Rikido Sato. Kaminari's implication wasn't unfounded, since Minoru Mineta was a sexual assault lawsuit waiting to happen, prone as he was to peeping, groping, and more. But at the moment, their problematic classmate was, indeed, taking a bath.

"Not Mineta! It was just for a sec, but I saw this creepy smiling face outside the window!" said Hagakure, with notes of both terror and fury in her voice. The invisible girl's T-shirt sleeve pointed toward the window to one side of the front door.

The boys gasped, realizing that if it really hadn't been Mineta, then the peeper wasn't a member of their class. Besides which, all of class 1-A was already inside for the night.

A villain, perhaps?

These kids had tangled with villains several times since school had begun, so one couldn't blame them for jumping to that hasty, frightening conclusion.

"What's up, guys?"

Eijiro Kirishima was about to take a bath himself, but he noticed his friends looking ill at ease. Izuku Midoriya, Tenya Ida, and Shoto Todoroki were drawn over by the commotion too. After a quick description of the peeping incident, they grew just as concerned about potential villainy.

"We ought to contact Aizawa Sensei posthaste," suggested Ida, but no sooner had the words left his mouth than they heard a series of sharp knocks on the front door. The group flinched, ready to fight or flee. No time to get word to their teacher. They glanced at each other and nodded before surrounding the entryway.

"Who is it?" Ida called out, looking nervous. No answer. Ida paused and turned to his classmates with a look that seemed to ask, "Should I open it?" Wordless, fearful nods in unison. Ida gripped the handle. The kids shifted into attack stances, ready to repel the threat on the other side of the door.

"Huhh? A guest shows up on your doorstep, and you people treat him like a common villain needing to be fought off? Honestly, class A, not very heroic of you! Ha ha ha ha!"

The group might have actually preferred a villain, because the quip and piercing laugh came from none other than Neito Monoma of class B, who ignored their dumbfounded looks and waltzed into the building.

"Hang on, was that you peeping through the window before, Monoma?" gasped Hagakure.

Monoma didn't answer straightaway, choosing instead to glance around the interior while oohing and ahhing. A grin rose on his face.

"Now that's just unwarranted slander. I was simply checking if anyone was home."

"Then you do admit to being our Peeping Tom?" questioned Ida, but Monoma ignored the valid point.

"How about…you just tell us why you're here?" said Izuku, realizing that the semantic argument was getting them nowhere fast.

"Am I not allowed to drop by without a reason?"

"I mean, sure, I guess, but…"

There was no besting Monoma when he was in one of his moods. Satisfied with the minor torment he'd already inflicted, he threw the class A kids a bone.

"I came to inspect, if you must know. I was wondering, perhaps, if our respective dorms differ in any way."

"Course they're not different. All the dorms got built exactly the same, man," said Kaminari, stepping forward from the puzzled group to counter Monoma's outrageous theory. He was right, of course—the buildings were identical in every way except for the massive signs over the front doors displaying 1-A, 1-B, and so on.

"Hah," came Monoma's quick deflection. "Have any of you even been to the other dorms?"

They shook their heads, conceding the point.

"Then how can you declare such a thing with such confidence?"

"Admittedly, we cannot…" said Ida.

"In that case," said a triumphant Monoma, "you'll have to let me check, just to be sure! Right? Right?"

UA

"Utter fanboy!"

"Sure. That's fair," said Midoriya.

"My eyes, they're blinded!"

"Merci, ☆" said Aoyama.

Monoma's cutting remarks followed quick visits to two of the boys' rooms on the second floor. Midoriya had already received the "fanboy" evaluation from his classmates back on move-in day, and Aoyama had purposely decorated his room to be blindingly sparkly, so neither was fazed by the obvious insults.

Having bullied his way into receiving permission to "inspect," Monoma had surveyed the common areas on the first floor before proceeding upstairs. Helpless in the face of his advance, the group that had met him at the door had followed along and, upon reaching Aoyama's room, discovered their glamorous classmate admiring himself in the mirror. Mineta, Fumikage Tokoyami, Katsuki Bakugo, Mezo Shoji, Hanta Sero, and Koji Koda were all relaxing in the bath—none the wiser to this invasion of privacy—so their rooms remained locked and safe from the impromptu inspection.

"*Sigh*... Just about what I expected, and therefore dull," declared Monoma as he walked down the hall, looking positively bored despite the grand tour being his idea in the first place.

"Dull, you say? Why must dorm rooms be interesting? They ought to be places equipped with practical necessities and nothing more. Isn't that enough?" said Ida.

Monoma's shrug seemed to mock Ida's straight-edged confusion.

"Nonsense. One's room is the ultimate representation of personal taste and style. The room reveals your true nature for all to see," said Monoma.

"Then it is my nature to be sparkling, *oui*? You were not wrong, ☆" said Aoyama, looking especially satisfied. Beside him, Midoriya's face twisted a bit.

"So deep down...I'm just a fanboy...?"

To Midoriya, *fanboy* meant somebody following

his dreams, so he wasn't about to protest the label. Still, he wasn't sure if he wanted that to constitute his entire identity. His friends all nodded at him, though, confirming that they knew him as a fanboy who ate, slept, and breathed everything hero related.

They moved on to the third floor, which featured Kaminari's, Ida's, and Ojiro's rooms.

"Check mine out!" said Kaminari as he swung open his door, eager to show off. Contrary to Kaminari's hopes, the skateboard, dartboard, speaker system, funky lamp in the corner, and various knickknacks displayed around the room had failed to impress the girls during the exhibition contest on move-in day. Girls just couldn't understand his style, he thought, but—pain in the butt or not—maybe Monoma had an eye for these things.

"Such an unsightly mishmash! It's exhausting on the eyes! There's plenty to appreciate but no cohesive theme," said Monoma, shattering Kaminari's hope with a brutal evaluation.

Ida's room came next. The unusual number of eyeglasses on display piqued Monoma's interest, but the rest of the room earned a brusque "Too stuffy and serious." Then they stopped by Ojiro's room, which contained only the bare necessities without making any sort of statement. It was perfect for an impromptu viewing, as inoffensive as a model room at a furniture store.

"A room this plain... It almost loops back around to being impressive," said Monoma, as if he'd stumbled upon something rare.

"Is that what everyone thinks of me, seriously...?" said Ojiro, slumping. He'd received the same assessment from the girls during the move-in day competition.

On the fourth floor, only Kirishima's room was available for viewing.

"I kinda doubt a dude like you would get it, but my room's totally manly!"

Monoma scanned the room, noticed the punching bag and inspirational posters, pulled out his phone without a word, fiddled with it for a moment, and turned the screen toward Kirishima. The photo showed a room with a punching bag, weight training equipment, and similar posters.

"When'd you snap a pic of my pad...?" asked Kirishima.

"This is Tetsutetsu's," explained Monoma.

"You're kidding? We've even got the same room!"

Kirishima had been less than thrilled when he'd learned that his Quirk and personality were nearly identical to those of Tetsutetsu Tetsutetsu, a boy in class B, so this didn't exactly help matters.

"Take a closer look," said Monoma. "Tetsutetsu's curtains are made of an especially heavy metal!"

"The dude's working on those gains every time he opens the curtains, even...?"

Monoma surveyed the shocked looks and gave a haughty snort.

"We in class B are always putting in that extra effort behind the scenes! Still, I can't say I'm surprised that class A is resting on its laurels, thinking of these dorm rooms as places to kick back and take a load off! So indulgent, so undisciplined! Before you know it, class B will be doing laps around y—"

"The only one who's gonna do laps is you, as punishment."

A swift chop to the back of the neck interrupted Monoma's mad rant, courtesy of Itsuka Kendo, the president of class B. The boy's knees buckled, but before he could slump to the ground, Kendo grabbed him by the collar. Behind them stood Tetsutetsu and class B's resident American, the large-horned Pony Tsunotori. Both looked just as troubled as Kendo.

"What's the big idea, Monoma?" said Tetsutetsu.

"I was very shocked when Monoma said he would visit class A tonight," said Tsunotori.

Apparently, Tsunotori had informed Kendo of Monoma's plan, so the leader of class B had taken it upon herself to retrieve the troublemaker. Despite the two dorm buildings being side by side, Tetsutetsu had decided to come along so the girls wouldn't have to walk alone in the dark.

"For the hundredth time, we're really sorry about Monoma," said Kendo. The group had moved back down to the first floor, where Kendo now forced Monoma's head forward into an apologetic bow.

"Don't interfere, Kendo. I was scouting for weaknesses to exploit," said Monoma, clearly not in a penitent mood.

"Scouting? Hang on, you said before you were inspecting," said Kaminari the instant Monoma had exposed his true intentions. The latter slipped out of Kendo's grip, defiant.

"Hmph. I dropped by to hang out, and you people didn't even put out tea. Class A just keeps showing its true colors!"

"Now it's 'hanging out,' huh? Ugh, you keep changing your story," said Kaminari.

"Such a will of steel..." remarked Midoriya, sounding impressed.

"Ah, how could I forget!" said Momo Yaoyorozu with a gasp, before marching off to the kitchen with Sato. Nearby, Kirishima and Tetsutetsu were having an animated conversation.

"Dude, I love how you incorporated curtains into your routine! Shoulda figured!"

"And your punching bag looks like it's taken a beating over the years, Kirishima! I knew I had you pegged as a man's man for a good reason!" fired back Tetsutetsu. They bumped fists.

UA

It wasn't long before Yaoyorozu and Sato returned to the group with tea and cake.

"Sato has prepared some sweets, and the tea is my personal blend. We hope it's to your liking," said Yaoyorozu, setting down the cups and saucers she had brought and decided to keep at Heights Alliance just for guests. The tea was deep red yet perfectly clear, hinting at a pure flavor unclouded by impurities.

"This's lemon chiffon," said Sato, pointing to the soft, pale yellow cake. "And the whipped cream's got hints of honey—the perfect pick-me-up after a long day of classes," added Sato.

"You seriously made this, Sato?" asked a wide-eyed Tetsutetsu.

"It looks so yummy!" said Tsunotori.

Beside them, Kendo looked around at the members of class A with a pained expression.

"You really shouldn't have, especially after Monoma barged his way in here..."

"Nonsense. You are our very first guests here, so

this is no more than should be expected. Please, enjoy," said Yaoyorozu.

"Really? Well…if you insist."

Urged by Yaoyorozu, the visitors tried the cake.

"Yum!" said Kendo.

"I don't usually go for sweets, but damn, this is tasty!" said Tetsutetsu.

"The cake and tea are perfect together!" added Tsunotori.

While his classmates raved about the offerings, Monoma looked like he was swallowing a bitter pill rather than fine tea and sweet cake.

"There was hardly a reason to go all out like this…" he grumbled, glaring at his portion though unable to find a word of legitimate criticism. He couldn't stop eating, either. With the harsh room review fresh in his mind, Kaminari didn't miss a chance to stick it to Monoma.

"So Sato's cake has got you beat, huh!" he cackled.

"Why should I care what you think, given your taste in interior decorating?" said Monoma, still on top of his game.

Kaminari snapped. "You sure talk big considering

we haven't even seen your room! If it turns out to be super lame, I'll never let you hear the end of it!"

"And if it isn't lame? What will you do?"

"I'll, uh, boil your tea water with my Quirk... No, wait, I'll use my electricity to heat class B's baths!"

Monoma whipped out his phone and showed Kaminari a photo.

"Here. My room."

Kaminari was at a loss for words, and a few other members of class A shifted around to get a look.

"So totally stylish!" said Hagakure, shocked.

The photo showed pastel walls complemented by tasteful white antique furniture, all perfectly coordinated to achieve a superb sense of unity. There was something vaguely French about it, to the point that nobody would've been surprised to spot the Eiffel Tower just outside Monoma's window.

"Seriously cute!" added Hagakure.

"You've done a lovely job with your room, I must say," said Yaoyorozu.

Kaminari slumped, realizing he couldn't find reasonable fault with the stylish room.

"Well? When will you be dropping by to heat our

baths? Don't overdo it, now—we wouldn't want you shocking us!" said Monoma, practically snorting in triumph.

"That's enough out of you," said Kendo, delivering another chop to Monoma's neck.

"Hey, hey, what's your room like, Kendo?" asked an excited Hagakure.

"M-mine?" stammered Kendo. Tsunotori decided to answer for her.

"Kendo's room is very cool! She has an old wooden table and black steel furniture. Also, a picture of a motorcycle."

"I ain't ashamed to admit that hers might even be manlier than mine," said Tetsutetsu, nodding.

"That bad, huh? Cutesy decorations just don't make me feel at home, I guess," said Kendo, looking awkward.

"How about your room, Tsunotori?" asked Yaoyorozu.

"My room...looks like this," said Tsunotori with a hint of embarrassment in her voice. The picture on her phone showed a room with anime posters and figures covering every spare surface.

"I love Japanese anime! Japanese culture is the best!"

"Ooh, I see you're a fan of one of my faves—*Cutie Ninja Shinobi*!" squealed Hagakure.

"Do you like that one too?" said Tsunotori. "When I was little, I used to pretend I was Shinobi all the time! 'Sneaky, stealthy Shinobi, go!'"

She struck a dynamic pose and made Hagakure's invisible eyes sparkle with joy.

"'Sneaking into your heart!'" said Hagakure, picking up the cue.

"'Cutie Ninja Shinobi is on the scene! Nin-nin-ninja!'" said the two giggling girls in unison, finishing off the tagline. Beside them, Midoriya couldn't take his eyes off the photo.

"What on earth is the matter, Midoriya? Why are you staring so intently?" asked Ida.

"You'll hurt your eyes that way," added Todoroki.

Too distracted to respond to his concerned friends, Midoriya swiveled his gaze up to Tsunotori's face.

"That. There. In the picture... Is that really the limited edition cowboy All Might figure, never released in Japan?"

"Oh. Yes, it is. I love All Might too!" replied Tsunotori.

"Too awesome! I knew they were selling that overseas, but I could never get my hands on one! Oh, um, could I stop by at some point to, uhh, take a few pictures?"

"Of course you can!"

"Ahh, thanks a million!" said Midoriya practically with tears in his eyes, ever the fanboy.

UA

Monoma watched bitterly as the entire group got along famously.

"Come on, time to go. Wouldn't want to overstay our welcome," he said, standing up suddenly.

Without a word of thanks for the tea and cake that he'd polished off, he marched toward the front door, only to have Kaminari and Ojiro cut him off.

"Whoaaa, there. You stomp around like you own the place, criticize our rooms, eat our cake, drink our tea, and now you wanna go home…? Nah, you've had your way, but I think it's our turn now. Right, Ojiro?" said Kaminari.

"Right. We haven't forgotten all that stuff you said…" added Ojiro.

"No, no, no, that wasn't criticism. I was just stating things objectively," said Monoma flatly, but they weren't having it.

"Stating the facts, huh? That's just a fancy way of insulting us even worse!" said Kaminari.

"What's so wrong with being plain? Everything that's plain and ordinary provides a standard to work off of!" said Ojiro.

Monoma had hurt their pride, so these boys were like wounded beasts who wouldn't back down, or perhaps a pair of grumpy kittens attempting to scratch back. It wasn't every day that class A went out of its way to engage with Monoma, though, and he was all too happy to take the bait and then some.

"Huhh? What do you propose we do about this? You won't let me leave, so you must have something in mind, right? A competition of sorts? A way to separate wheat from chaff? To determine once and for all which class is superior?"

Monoma's rivals—the ones he loved to hate and hated to love—were, for a change, having a go at him. Kendo attempted to halt the brewing storm, but her protests fell on deaf ears.

"Some sorta contest? Sure! Assuming you're not chicken!" said Kaminari.

"Why would the inevitable winner be chicken, pray tell?" boasted Monoma.

"Will the two of you behave yourselves, please!" said Ida, stepping between the boys. "Surely you realize we aren't allowed to compete inside the dormitory?"

Monoma's eyes gleamed; he wasn't about to allow the uptight Ida to stop a potential showdown.

"You're president of class A, so don't tell me you've forgotten which school we're at. This is U.A., friend! That Plus Ultra mentality is all about overcoming the obstacles in our path, yes?"

"Hrm, you mean to say…that we should engender that spirit of constant improvement, even in our residence halls? That healthy competition will only propel us to greater heights…? Yes, of course, I understand!" exclaimed Ida.

Having dealt with Ida handily, Monoma turned back to Kaminari and Ojiro with a look of triumph on his face.

"What sort of contest shall it be, then? I'm ready for any challenge you decide to bring!"

"Um… Errr… I dunno?"

Kaminari couldn't think of anything. He turned to Ojiro for assistance.

"How about…arm wrestling…?" suggested Ojiro, not sounding very confident.

"Huhh? A grudge match in the wake of our tournament at training camp? How utterly uninspired!"

"S-sumo, then!"

"Swapping one sort of wrestling for another? Bah. Besides, do I look like a muscle-bound brute to you?"

"Hey, man, didn't you say 'any challenge'? If you're so picky, then you decide!" said Kaminari.

"Relinquishing the decision to me, when you're the one who threw down the gauntlet? Really?" said Monoma.

"You're the one always challenging us, though! Guess this means you can't think of anything either!" shot back Kaminari.

The rest of group stood back in stunned silence, watching the argument heat up as every proposal was shot down by Monoma for one reason or another. Todoroki remembered something and gasped softly.

"What is it, Todoroki?" asked Ida.

"If it's a competition we need, I might have just the thing."

UA

Todoroki returned from his room with the barrel-shaped toy. Everyone present recognized the design, which featured slots around the circumference and a hole on top. Players would take turns sticking swords into the slots, only one of which would trigger the pirate emerging from the barrel to fully pop out, determining the loser of the game. A popular and beloved classic.

"Oh, the good old Pirate Panic game, huh!" said Kaminari, who wasn't the only one grinning at the sight of the familiar toy.

"I wouldn't expect you to have such a thing, Todoroki," said Yaoyorozu.

"Someone gave it to me," said Todoroki, offering no further explanation.

"Was the pirate-in-a-barrel game always so big, though?" wondered Ojiro with a tilt of his head. The classic design they all remembered from childhood was small enough to grab with one hand, but this barrel was as big as a basketball. Still, they were too caught up in the moment to give it much thought.

"Must be the deluxe edition! And the perfect way to settle our score, yeah?" said Kaminari eagerly.

"Yes, the time has come to see whether fate will side with class A or B!" said Monoma, actually agreeing with a member of class A for a change.

They settled on the rules of their bout; turns would alternate between classes A and B, and whichever class inserted the losing sword and produced the pop-up pirate would lose. Both classes furnished teams of two boys and two girls each, since that was all class B had to offer. Representing class A were Kaminari and Ojiro (out to avenge their honor), an excitable Hagakure, and Mina Ashido, who'd just wandered over after finishing her bath. Monoma won a quick round of rock-paper-scissors against Kaminari, so he got to decide which class would stick in the first sword.

"Ha ha ha ha ha! As expected, Lady Luck is on class B's side today!" cackled Monoma more triumphantly that the minor victory warranted.

"Hurry up and choose, you!" said Ashido, eager to get started.

None of the spectators nor even the class B members who'd been drawn into Monoma's shenanigans managed

to summon quite the same enthusiasm. After all, this grand showdown would be decided over a children's game.

"In that case, I will take a stab at drawing first blood!" declared Monoma.

He picked a slot and inserted one of the toy swords. The onlookers heard a mechanism click within, then a violent buzzing as electricity flowed through Monoma's body via the sword. He let out a voiceless scream and collapsed on the table, twitching and smoldering. The stunned silence was broken by Tetsutetsu.

"Monoma, you okay, man? Speak to me! Stay with us!"

"Don't plan my funeral just yet..." muttered Monoma. He summoned enough strength to turn toward Kaminari.

"A sneaky zap attack? Well played, you... I didn't think class A could get any bolder, yet here we are!"

"Hang on, I didn't do nothing! You were all watching, right? Vouch for me!" said Kaminari, desperate to clear himself of suspicion.

"No, he's right," said Ojiro, still shocked by the turn of events. "The zap came from the barrel itself."

"So Monoma picked the losing slot, I guess?"

"That's how this game works, really?"

"But the pirate didn't pop out…"

"I don't get it."

The emergence of the pirate normally indicated the loser of the game, but Monoma's stab hadn't triggered it. In the confusion, Midoriya turned to Todoroki.

"Why don't we check the instruction booklet, if you've got it…?"

"I don't," came Todoroki's characteristically blunt reply, though the look on his face showed that he was shaken too. With a scowl, he explained.

"I got this thing from that Hatsume girl in the Support Course. She made it herself. Wanted us to play and give her feedback, or something…"

"Whaaat?"

"Come again?"

As former victims of Hatsume's support items, both Midoriya and Ida yelped at the sound of her name. Hatsume was more passionate about her inventions than anything, and giving this particular "baby" to Todoroki was her way of rewarding him for his help and conducting a test run of a tool meant to fluster villains.

"Sorry…" mumbled Todoroki. He hadn't been expecting a torture device.

"Maybe we should call it quits?" suggested Midoriya nervously. "This is Hatsume we're talking about, so who knows what other sorts of tricks she's stuffed in there…"

"I am in complete agreement! Far better to quit while we're ahead!" said Ida.

Not everyone in the group had met Hatsume, but she was already infamous enough by reputation.

"True enough," said Kendo. "No reason to purposely put ourselves in harm's way… How about we put our competition on hold?"

"Huhh?"

Monoma wasn't having it.

"Ridiculous! One shocking development isn't enough to make me turn tail…"

"You're, uh, not looking so hot, though," pointed out Kendo.

As Monoma attempted to smooth down his newly frizzy do, he spotted Kaminari looking distressed—worried, even.

"Unless you're ready to throw in the towel?" he said with a provocative sidelong glance. "Is a child's game too much for poor class A to handle? Sorry for not

realizing sooner! It didn't occur to me that underneath all that bravado, you were quaking in your boots! But no, go ahead—slink up to your rooms and cry about it in bed like the pathetic losers you are!"

"As if! We're gonna keep playing!" shouted Kaminari. He'd bought the fight Monoma was hawking, and despite the others' concern, there was no return policy on this one. Even as the only actual victim so far, Monoma couldn't back down either; his pride was worth a little pain. Death before dishonor, and all.

"We're still in this, right, Ojiro?" said Kaminari.

"Um. Right."

Monoma's electrocution had put a damper on Ojiro's competitive spirit, but he couldn't bring himself to disappoint Kaminari.

"But you girls don't have to if you don't want to…" said Ojiro.

"What're you talking about, Ojiro?" said Hagakure. "We gotta see this through to the end!"

"And I actually kinda love torture games like this!" added Ashido.

"You're a great couple of gals!" said Kaminari, practically moved to tears by his teammates' enthusiasm. Seeing this, Tsunotori clenched her fists and smiled at her own teammates.

"I will play too! I saw this game in an anime! I always wanted to play it!"

"Count me in too, then. Wouldn't want to leave our team one player short," said Kendo. It was Tetsutetsu's turn to be moved.

"Lookit that!" he said, gripping Monoma's shoulder and jostling him about amicably. "We got ourselves two full teams of willing contenders for a true-blue bout!"

Monoma felt a bit awkward in the face of Tetsutetsu's pure intentions, so he grimaced, shook himself lose, and pointed a toy sword straight at team A.

"Time for your team to feel the pain! Who's the next victim?"

"Me!" said Kaminari, swiping the sword from Monoma's hand.

"You eat voltage for breakfast, though! How is that fair?" said Monoma, looking resentful.

"Hey, man, nothing I can do about the Quirk I was born with!"

Deep down, Kaminari knew it was unfair, but he didn't care. In fact, he would welcome a quick charge

of his batteries. He picked a slot and inserted his sword, but the zap he expected never came. For half a second, the players and onlookers alike were convinced that the toy must've malfunctioned during Monoma's turn, but that was a fleeting hope. In an instant, part of the barrel transformed into bindings that locked Kaminari's arms in place before a pair of robotic fingers extended and smacked him across his wrists. He screamed, the rest of the group gaped, and the barrel returned to its original compact form with a whir.

"That was like...*shippe*, right? That smack on the wrists for monks who get distracted when meditating..." said Sato, sending Midoriya into one of his muttering monologues.

"Electrocution, shippe... Both common punishments in these sorts of torture games. I guess Hatsume designed this so that each sword triggers some sort of painful response... Maybe a different one for each slot? Since I doubt Hatsume would be satisfied with a lack of variety..."

"We're seriously gonna get brutalized in a different way every turn?" said Kaminari, on the verge of tears after hearing Midoriya's analysis.

"And that's why she had to make the barrel so much bigger than usual," said Ojiro understandingly. Even the threat of a cornucopia of punishments couldn't stop the group's momentum at this point, though.

"Bring it on, torture barrel!" said Tetsutetsu. "I'm ready for ya!"

His sword sunk into a slot as he finished his battle cry, and a long stick with a rubber band on the end emerged, stopping just in front of his face. The device drew back the rubber band and released, making it snap against Tetsutetsu's forehead with a loud plink.

"Hmph," he grunted, unhurt, since he had activated his skin-hardening Quirk, "Steel," just before impact.

"Hey, talk about unfair!" yelped Kaminari.

Monoma cast him a cynical grin. "I seem to remember somebody explaining how there's nothing unfair about the Quirks we're born with."

Kaminari gave a frustrated grumble, and beside him, Ojiro timidly picked up a sword.

"My turn now, I guess..." he said, selecting a slot. Another rod popped out—this one with a slim strip of something or other on the end.

"Duct tape? How would that inflict pain?" wondered Midoriya.

The rod extended toward Ojiro and stuck the piece of tape to the especially fluffy tip of his tail, which was curled around in front of him.

"Oh no... Hang on! Don't!"

Despite Ojiro's protest, the unfeeling machine ripped the tape away, taking a chunk of fur with it. As Ojiro clutched his tail and writhed in pain, a trembling Midoriya muttered, "It must go for leg hair, usually..." The mundane but intense torture would presumably be effective no matter which exposed body part was chosen.

"I'm next..." said Kendo, looking determined and ready for anything, but her sword's stab didn't seem to have any effect. As she leaned closer to the barrel, it shot a puff of something in her face.

"Yeesh, that reeks!"

Her face puckered at a stench she might have described as hot, rotting garbage wrapped in a milk-soaked rag and left to stew in a locker for a humid week in summer. On instinct, she activated her Quirk, "Big Fist," and tried to wave away the smell using her gigantic hand as a fan. Naturally, this only made it spread about the space, eliciting disgusted cries from the whole group.

"Ack, sorry, guys!"

Though still reeling, Hagakure steeled herself, said, "My turn!" and stuck a sword into the barrel. Two arms popped out and began tickling her aggressively. As she giggled uncontrollably, her T-shirt and shorts writhed around violently in midair.

"Now it is my turn..." said Tsunotori with trepidation. Her sword summoned another arm—one that stuck a small green blob directly into her mouth. A few seconds later, her eyes started watering and she clamped her hands over her nose.

"Nose! Burning!"

"That must have been wasabi!" said Yaoyorozu, putting two and two together.

"Oh, so this is the famous wasabi!" said Tsunotori, clearly excited to be experiencing more Japanese culture, despite the extreme discomfort.

Ashido was up next, and she gulped as she inserted her sword. A new mechanical arm stuck a transparent lump down the back of her shirt.

"Eeek, that's cold!"

While Hagakure struggled to get the piece of ice out from under her friend's shirt, Izuku began muttering again.

"Incredible! This torture game isn't just about physical pain, but also incorporates smell, taste, and other sensations, with every punishment different than the last, so we never know what's coming! I wonder what awaits the actual loser of the game...?"

Everyone gasped at Midoriya's implication; if even the "safe" slots had such brutal surprises in store, what had Hatsume prepared for the one losing position? The very question filled them with dread.

"Feel free to cry uncle now, Monoma..." said Kaminari.

"Hah. Funny. Projecting much?" said Monoma.

Neither would budge. For the young and stupid, there was no turning back, even in the face of danger.

All eight players had gone once, so it was again Monoma's turn. Round two featured a forehead flick, a frying pan to the head, a cream pie to the face, an exploding balloon, and more. Every slot they filled inflicted some sort of damage, making them wonder with increasing trepidation how it could possibly get worse.

UA

At long last, only two slots remained, so one had to be the loser.

"Here I go!" cried Ashido, pumping herself up.

Her sword went in, and an arm popped out that grabbed her and swung her about. When the arm had released Ashido and she'd stopped shrieking, a worried Yaoyorozu asked, "Are you all right?"

"Yeah. Fun. Kinda felt like break-dancing, actually," said Ashido matter-of-factly.

The pirate was still lodged in his barrel, which told the players that the final slot must be the losing one. Based on turn order, the inevitable loser would be Monoma.

"Class A's gonna win this thing!" said Kaminari triumphantly. "Unless you're too scared?" This prompted a grunt and a scowl from his rival.

"So petty, so cruel! Is that any way for a future hero to act? Our loss is set in stone, so isn't that enough for you? I mean, what a bully! Are you sure your career path won't lead you to villainy instead? How horrible! We've got a wolf in sheep's clothing, here! A villain in the making!"

"Yeah, yeah. You're just scared of taking your lumps," said Kaminari.

"You've been anything but sportsmanlike up to now, so this change of attitude isn't fooling anyone..." added Ojiro. They understood Monoma's fear of whatever the final torture might be, but neither was willing to play by his rules anymore.

"You're honestly going to make me do this? How about an apology instead? I'm sooo sorry. How's that? Enough for you? I knew this game would reveal class A's true nature! Try having a heart!"

"Stop embarrassing yourself," said Kendo, striking at Monoma's neck from above with the side of her hand. Before he could collapse in a heap, an enraged Tetsutetsu grabbed him by the collar.

"Not manly at all, Monoma!"

"Why should I pretend I'm eager and willing? Think what you will of me, but I refuse to finish this game!" shouted Monoma, his defiant speech actually coming off as manly, in a strange way.

"If you're so scared, I'll take your turn for you!" said Tetsutetsu, who couldn't take any more of Monoma's shameful display.

"Huh? You will?"

"Yeah, cuz a man's word is his bond!"

As Tetsutetsu picked up the final sword, Kirishima—with tears in his eyes—said, "Now there's a man's man!"

"Here I go," said Tetsutetsu resolutely.

The sword went in, and with bated breath, everyone stiffened up on instinct, ready for the worst. They'd never felt so focused—even during class. There would have been less tension in the air if they'd been facing down an unknown villain in a dark alley.

The click of the final mechanism echoed through the room.

Then, a dry pop, as the toy pirate finally shot out of the barrel, accompanied by a burst of colorful confetti and a recording of Hatsume's cheery voice.

"Congratulations!"

Everyone was dumbfounded, and Midoriya gasped.

"Hatsume designed it so whoever makes the pirate pop out is the winner! Actually, I remember hearing that that's how the original game was meant to be before they put it on the market..."

The group flew into a rage upon hearing Midoriya's analysis.

"Hang on, so who's the winner?" asked Hagakure.

"Why, class B of course! It was Tetsutetsu who produced the pirate!" declared Monoma.

"No freaking way! We decided at the start that whoever made the pirate pop would lose!" said Kaminari, getting fired up again.

"And we just had to take all those horrible punishments in the meantime…" said Kendo. This brought the boys to their senses, since just thinking back on the series of tortures left them exhausted.

"No. Yeah. We're going home," conceded Monoma.

Though they'd stormed in earlier like a surprise squall, the four members of class B now stumbled to the entryway, where class A saw them off and breathed sighs of relief once the door was shut.

"Block parties can be hell," said Kaminari with gravitas.

"Only Monoma. The rest of them aren't so bad," pointed out Ojiro fairly.

The weary members of class A grinned at each other, knowing full well that this wouldn't be the last run-in with their new neighbors at U.A. High.

Part 4
The Hundred Tales of U.A.

G rim faces and deer skulls—illuminated only by eerie candlelight—seemed to float in a circle, as if participants in some demonic summoning ritual.

"Of course the man was terrified," said Hanta Sero. "But he couldn't exactly turn back now, so he kept making his way down the dark tunnel, one trembling step at a time... Right when he'd made it halfway, through, a warm puff of air tickled his throat. This was odd, since there shouldn't have been any wind blowing from up ahead."

Sero was really selling his story.

"W-why not...?" asked Denki Kaminari with an anxious gulp.

"Because the tunnel had been a dead end ever since the year before, when a landslide had caused a cave-in."

"No way…" muttered Mina Ashido, astonishment painted all over her face. Sero glanced around at his captive audience and went on in a whisper.

"The man stopped for a second and felt something drip on his hand. Something cold. He'd been careful about not draining the batteries of his flashlight, but the dripping didn't stop, so he turned it on and shone the beam of light directly above. That's when he saw it… A blood-soaked corpse!" said Sero, his voice rising for the story's shocking ending.

"Gahhhh!" cried Minoru Mineta as he scrambled to grab ahold of one of Mezo Shoji's massive arms, like a koala wrapping itself around a tree.

Next to Shoji, Tsuyu Asui spoke in her typical flat tone. "Quiet down, Mineta."

"Seriously!" agreed a grumpy Ashido through pursed lips. "Your screaming killed the scary factor, Mineta!"

Still clinging to Shoji and with tears in his eyes, Mineta shot back.

"H-how're you girls not scared? Girls are s'posed to be wimpy and all!"

"That's big talk, coming from the screaming guy

who's grabbing on to a big, strong man!" mocked Sero, but Mineta dug his heels in.

"Can't help it! Your story was just too spooky!"

The kids were getting used to dorm life, and on this particular Sunday, resident party animals Sero, Ashido, and Kaminari had decided to get together for a scary-story session. They'd also invited Shoji and Asui to join the fun.

"Why'd you even wanna be here, then?" asked Sero.

An enraged yet still terrified Mineta struggled to find a retort, but Asui poked her head around Shoji and answered for him.

"If I know Mineta, he was hoping to grope us in the dark."

They all knew well enough by this point that their tiniest classmate was the embodiment of lust itself, so rather than seat him next to the girls, the group had sandwiched him between Shoji and Kaminari.

"C'mon, men are basically treasure hunters, always looking out for a lucky-perv chance!" declared Mineta, implicitly admitting that Asui had hit the nail on the head.

"Don't lump the rest of us men in with you," said Shoji through a mouth on one of his dupli-arm tentacles.

"What a creep! Good thing we'll finally be able to take our baths with peace of mind, starting today," said Ashido with a smile.

"Agreed. That will be a relief," added Asui.

Mineta realized what they meant and grimaced.

"Tch. Damn that chick from the Support Course with the sweet rack... Sticking her nose where it doesn't belong!"

The girls of class 1-A had all agreed that they couldn't live with the threat of Mineta peeping every time they bathed, so they'd gone to Mei Hatsume and asked for an anti-peeping security item to place at the entrance to the girls' bathing area—something that was sure to keep a certain creeper from sneaking in.

"Oh, I know!" said Ashido. "Let's go back to Hatsume and have her whip up a 'stop Mineta from groping us in dark rooms' item!"

"Nooo! You're killing off all my lucky-perv chances, one by one!"

"Enough..." said a voice from the corner. "Or else find another room for your antics..."

Fumikage Tokoyami sat in a chair outside the story circle with a clear scowl on his beaked face. The gang had decided that his room was the best setting for spooky stories, so Tokoyami was now part of this whether he liked it or not.

"But this's the only pitch-black spot at this time of day! Plus, you've got skulls and stuff to set the mood!" said Ashido with a grin and a thumbs-up.

The skulls were purely decorative, of course, but they could've been mistaken for real bones in the dim candlelight.

"I didn't furnish my room with you people and your ghost stories in mind!" said Tokoyami with another scowl.

"Pretty lucky that you had candles lying around too," added Ashido.

"Not lucky for me!"

"No, wait, I've got it! I'm about to tell a tale so spooky it'll scare the feathers right offa you, Tokoyami!" said Ashido, though her sunniness didn't seem to penetrate Tokoyami's dark mood.

UA

At that moment, Momo Yaoyorozu, Ochaco Uraraka, Toru Hagakure, and Kyoka Jiro were in Jiro's room on the third floor, where the latter was showing the rest of the girls a thing or two about playing music. Uraraka plucked a guitar string, producing a low tone.

"Ooh, I played a note!"

Next to her, Yaoyorozu also had a guitar in hand.

"How does one hold a pick properly, Jiro?" she asked.

"Just how you've got it. And the movement's all in the elbow and wrist."

"Listen to, like, the wailing of my soul!" cried Hagakure as she dove into an ambitious solo on air guitar.

But learning guitar proved harder than expected, so the girls asked Jiro to give them a demonstration.

"Eh? Okay. Maybe just a short something or other," said Jiro, obviously embarrassed. She took a deep breath, raised her pick, and proceeded to play a quick piece that involved some masterful finger work on the frets. The other three girls gaped in awe.

"Super rad!" said Ochaco.

"You're basically a pro!" said Hagakure.

"Encore, Jiro! Encore!" said Yaoyorozu.

"Aww, knock it off. Geez!"

The unexpected compliments turned Jiro's face several shades redder, but she went ahead and honored Yaoyorozu's request for an encore all the same.

UA

Outside, on the lawn in front of the dormitory, Izuku Midoriya was getting tips from Tenya Ida in the hope of adding some kicking moves to his repertoire.

"You won't achieve speed or power by moving your legs alone, Midoriya. Put your entire body into it... Now, observe once more!"

"Right! Let me see how it's done!" said Midoriya, who watched with wide eyes as Ida demonstrated a series of kicks. So as not to forget the nuances, he began scribbling in his notebook immediately.

"I see... He drops his hips nice and low for a firmer stance... Like his whole body is coiled up..."

"Oh. You guys. Hard at work, huh," said Shoto Todoroki, who'd just emerged from the front door.

"Heya, Todoroki. Leaving already?" said Midoriya.

Both he and Ida knew that if nothing else was going on, Todoroki was sure to visit his mother in the hospital on Sundays.

"Anyway, hope you have a good time!" added Midoriya.

"Give our best regards to your mother," said Ida.

"Sure. Thanks," said Todoroki as he set out.

As the two boys watched their friend fade from view, Midoriya gasped and said, "Sorry, Ida!"

"What for?" asked Ida, confused by the apology and the guilty look on Midoriya's face.

"Y'know, for asking you to spend your day off training with me. I didn't even ask if you had other plans already."

Ida let loose a deep laugh.

"Nonsense, Midoriya. You wished to learn, so I am here to teach. It's the very least I can do as class president and, more importantly, your friend. Besides which, it gives me great pride to assist someone I respect so much."

"Wow, Ida…" said Midoriya, matching Ida's wide smile.

"Let's try this again, shall we?"

"Sure!"

If this diligent pair had their way, they'd be training together from dawn to dusk.

UA

In Eijiro Kirishima's room on the fourth floor, Mashirao Ojiro was attacking all sides of the punching bag with his tail. As a martial artist, he'd taken immediate notice of Kirishima's punching bag and asked if he could smack it around a bit.

"This is great. It feels like I'm strengthening my whole body," said Ojiro.

"Right? The perfect way to train for dudes like us, who hit stuff!"

"Do you mind if I try kicking it?"

"Go ahead! Oh, but wait…"

Before Kirishima could mention that strong kicks tended to send the punching bag crashing to the floor, Ojiro's next attack did just that. Seconds later, the door to Kirishima's room slammed open.

"Thought I told you to pipe down in here!" yelled

Katsuki Bakugo, clearly fed up with the noise coming from next door, and not for the first time.

The fourth floor was having an action-packed Sunday as well.

Back in Tokoyami's room, Ashido was wrapping up her scary story.

"And then, the medium got the shock of her life, cuz, like, the closet was full of ghosts and stuff! Spooky, yeah?"

"Eek!" screamed Mineta, once again clinging to Shoji for dear life. But the rest of audience blinked blankly, plainly unimpressed.

"Wait. Was my story not scary?" asked Ashido.

"Not really," said Asui with a tilt of her head. "The story itself had potential, but not the way you told it, Mina."

"Right, if you're gonna tell a ghost story, you gotta use your voice to up the spooky factor, the way I did. You gotta be a performer, basically," said Sero with a haughty chuckle.

"For real. You've got the knack for making it real

hair-raising, Sero," said Kaminari, recalling how freaked out he'd been just a few minutes ago.

"What the heck!" said Ashido, pouting again. "That was the scariest one in my roster."

She paused a beat before her face lit up with a new idea.

"I know! How about a story from Tokoyami? I bet he's a master of horror!"

"Ooh, good idea!" agreed Kaminari. "Tokoyami's normal voice is already scary enough for this kinda thing."

"And what is that supposed to mean?" asked Tokoyami, not thrilled with Kaminari's assessment.

"I wouldn't mind a story from Tokoyami," said Asui.

"C'mon, horror master!" said Ashido.

"Not too scary, Tokoyami, okay…? Unless it's got some sexy parts. Then feel free to go nuts," said Mineta.

With all eyes and expectations on him, Tokoyami scrunched his face, sighed, and cleared his throat.

"The following is a story told to me by my grandfather when I was young. Maybe it will leave you all sufficiently terrified," he said, with the slightest hint of satisfaction in his voice.

"Many years ago, the youths in a certain village amused themselves with the Hundred Tales."

"I feel like I've heard of those, but what're the Hundred Tales about, again?" asked Kaminari flatly.

"It's a way of telling ghost stories, passed down through the ages," explained Shoji. "You light one hundred candles before starting and blow out one for every story you tell throughout the night. When the final candle goes out, they say a real ghost is supposed to show up."

"Ooh, we've got candles right here! Perfect for the Hundred Tales!" said Ashido, growing excited.

Tokoyami swiveled his chair toward the group and went on.

"In this particular village, the Hundred Tales was one of the few amusements these youths had available to them. Wary of summoning a real specter, they were always sure to stop at the ninety-ninth tale. One day, however, a blond woman came to the village from the city. As a world traveler, she had heard about the Hundred Tales and was eager to join the fun, so the youths happily welcomed her to their storytelling circle that night. Not one of their tales made her cry out in fright, though. In fact, partway through, she began to grin, which only served to frighten the youths. At last,

they got through ninety-nine tales and decided to stop, as always, but the visitor broke her silence and began to tell the one hundredth tale of the night. The group implored her to stop, but she did not. When her tale concluded, the final candle blew out all on its own."

"Probably just a breeze that did it, right?" said Sero, taking a stab at a logical explanation.

"S-so? Did a ghost appear...?" asked Ashido with a terrified gulp.

"One of the youths kept a brave face and pointed out that no ghost or ghoul had emerged, but when he tried to relight the candle...the blond woman had vanished altogether. The next morning, the entire village and its police force conducted a search, but she was nowhere to be found. Perhaps she'd simply gone home, some thought, while others whispered that maybe she had been spirited away. Time passed until most had forgotten about the blond woman, but one day, one of the youths present that fateful night claimed that he had spotted the woman again. The others were convinced his eyes had deceived him, until the next day when his body was discovered, his face twisted in an expression of sheer terror at the moment of death.

 SCHOOL BRIEFS

And wrapped around his neck? A single blond hair…"

"Yikes!" said Ashido, squirming timidly. She wrapped her own arms around one of Asui's and took refuge behind Shoji.

"What's up with you?" asked Kaminari.

"This position just makes me feel, I dunno, safer…?" said Ashido poking her face out from behind her large classmate.

"I get it. Shoji is big enough to feel like a protective dad or something," agreed Asui.

"I need some protection too, in that case," said Mineta, sensing a lucky-perv chance and scrambling toward the girls, but one of Shoji's arms held the boy back.

"The next day," Tokoyami went on, "another of the youths from that night turned up dead. Then another, and another, until everyone who had been present for the blond woman's hundredth tale was no more. The rest of the village was convinced that the woman must be a soul-sucking demon of some sort."

"Eh? Why'd they jump to the demon explanation?" asked Sero.

"Because of a certain legend in the village," explained Tokoyami. "Long, long ago, it was said, a local couple had given birth to a daughter with blond hair. The dark-haired husband assumed his wife had been unfaithful, and despite his wife's protests, he abandoned her and their newborn daughter on the mountainside. Deep in the mountains, the wife sacrificed the baby to a demon in order to lay a powerful, grudge-filled curse upon her cruel husband."

"So the baby turned into a demon and eventually came back to cause trouble...?" asked Asui, who felt Ashido's trembling grip tighten around her arm. "Or at least, that's what the villagers assumed, all those years later?"

Tokoyami nodded and glanced around the group.

"However, the story did not end there. The friend who told my grandfather this tale moved away from the village in question at a young age. As a grown man, he found himself nostalgic for his hometown, but when he returned for a visit, he found the village deserted and in ruins. According to those in the next town over, the village was afflicted by a terrible plague that killed off each and every resident. Was it really illness that destroyed them, though? Perhaps not, as

rumor has it that strands of blond hair were found near the bodies..."

"Okay, whoa. This is getting way too freaky for me!" said Ashido, tears forming in her eyes.

"Sero had more of a straightforward story, but this slowly gets worse and worse," said Asui, with a slight look of concern on her usual poker face.

"I'm afraid there is still more to come," said Tokoyami with a shake of his head after pausing for his listeners' comments.

"After the man returned from the ruined village and told my grandfather his story, he began acting strangely. Apparently, he had spotted the grinning blond woman and was now afraid that spreading word of her had cursed him too. 'Maybe you were just imagining things?' suggested my grandfather, but the friend was convinced. He died, suddenly, several days later, with a single strand of blond hair wrapped about his neck."

This final, terrifying development left the group aghast. With a strained smile, Sero rubbed his arms as if hit by sudden chills.

"This one's gonna keep me up tonight..." he said.

"This is fiction, yeah?" said a visibly frightened Kaminari, pressing Tokoyami. "Totally made up, right?"

Tokoyami seemed a bit flustered by his classmate's reactions.

"I apologize...if this was too scary. But no, my grandfather really told me this tale. As for whether or not he made it up? I cannot say."

"Shoji. Stand watch while I go pee, okay?" begged Mineta, tossing any notion of manly pride out the window.

"Your room's just down the hall. You'll be fine," said Shoji.

"Just stand outside the door while I go! C'mon!"

"The stories we pass down," said Tokoyami, eyes fixed on his audience, "contain lessons. The lesson of my tale is that stories themselves should be treated as more than mere amusements or ways to pass the time. Wandering, cursed spirits roam closer to home than we might expect, and they are always listening. Even here and now, perhaps..."

There was no levity in Tokoyami's concluding words. The group swallowed hard.

"Tokoyami is right. That seems like enough ghost stories for today," said Asui.

"Darn right! This just got a little too real," said Ashido, who seemed relieved, and Sero and Kaminari nodded in agreement.

"H-how about we forget the spooky stuff and go for pervy stories next time? I've even got some choice videos back in my room that we can have playing in the background!" said Mineta, his desperation palpable.

"No thanks," said the two girls in unison.

UA

Late that night, Mineta found himself tossing and turning. He'd tried falling asleep, but his mind kept drifting back to Tokoyami's story. He was regretting attending the storytelling circle in the first place, since he hadn't even pulled off the lucky-perv moment he'd been hoping for.

Suddenly, a small, sharp sound.

Mineta's eyes bulged, but when he realized it was just the creak of the dorm building as the temperature dropped, he breathed a sigh of relief and scolded himself for being so on edge. In this jumpy state, he knew that a pervy fantasy or two would be just the thing to help him settle down and fall asleep. But as he started pondering what to fantasize about...

A low buzz.

It was faint, clearly not the rattling of the building, and not coming from Midoriya's room next door. It was out in the hallway.

J-just my imagination!

The buzzing continued, louder than a moment ago. This was not in Mineta's head.

Aw, dammit...

Mineta decided to investigate, since there would be no fantasizing about anything if the noise kept up. He crept toward the door, cursing the noise for scaring him enough to disrupt his plans. Probably just one of his second-floor neighbors, out in the hall with a buzzing cell phone, right? That's what Mineta told himself as he pushed open the door.

The corridor was empty, though.

Mineta's face froze. He shut the door, made a beeline back to the bed, and dove under his blanket.

L-like I said, just my imagination! Nobody and nothing out there!

He poked his head out from under the blanket to make sure the noise was gone, but there it was again, getting still louder. Louder and closer.

Why would it be coming after me? *Naw, it's gotta be the vents in the building or something!*

Except the ventilation system had never made this sound before—a fact that Mineta tried desperately to bury deep and out of sight in his mind. The buzzing grew and grew until it stopped just outside his door.

In the next instant, a thumping knock against Mineta's door, and a woman's voice.

"Minoru... Mineta..."

"Gahhhhh!"

UA

During a break between classes the next day, the classroom was abuzz with talk of the buzzing in the night. It hadn't just been Mineta—Asui, Sero, Ashido, Kaminari, Tokoyami, and Shoji had also heard it.

"Why'd she only call out *our* names though? Please tell me one of you is lying and that it wasn't just our group specifically!" said Mineta, upon learning that the rest of the class hadn't received visits in the night.

"You seriously didn't hear anything, Midoriya?" he said, getting desperate.

"Sorry, but no! I was exhausted from training yesterday, so I fell right asleep..."

"Heh, if we're the only ones who heard it...maybe Tokoyami's tale really did curse us?" joked Sero.

"C-cut it out, man," said Kaminari. Both boys wore forced smiles.

"You guys really believe that?" said Rikido Sato with a laugh. "Sounds like that scary story has you imagining things!"

"N-not like we're *that* gullible, but it was super scary, okay? The blond ghost lady is no joke," shot back Kaminari. This caught Kirishima's interest.

"Ooh, so how'd this story go, exactly?" he asked.

"Well, first off..."

As Kaminari started to explain, Bakugo and Todoroki—both at their desks—took notice.

"Quit it with your weird-ass stories when I'm within

earshot!" shouted Bakugo, bolting up out of his chair. With hands in pockets, he slid open the classroom door with his foot—like always—and stormed out.

Maybe he scares easily...?

Midoriya kept this thought to himself, though.

Kyoka Jiro hadn't said a word until now, but she decided to speak up, her voice trembling.

"Um, I heard it too, actually. The strange buzzing... It kept going until dawn."

"There, see! It must've been real then," said Kaminari, grasping at that small triumph, though part of him still wished it had been their collective imaginations. For better or worse, Jiro was class 1-A's resident expert on all things sound related, so her word was as good as proof. An aura of unease settled over the entire class, and Ida stepped forward with his own commanding assessment.

"Curse or no curse, the fact that several of you heard this odd noise is concerning indeed. There may be something wrong with the dormitory itself, so we need to get to the bottom of this. As class president, I will take responsibility and solve this mystery!"

LAJ

That night, Ida sat outside his room in the hallway, wrapped in a blanket. He found himself fighting to keep awake, which was no surprise, as he was the type to adhere to a strict bedtime under ordinary circumstances.

"Oh my, almost nodded off again…" said Ida before taking a sip of the coffee prepared for him by the girls. Midoriya and some of the others had suggested they keep watch in shifts, but the class president had refused their offer, feeling that it was his duty to ensure a good night's sleep for his electorate. The coffee wasn't doing much to keep him awake, though.

Let's just hope that nothing comes of this.

As his eyelids started to close, Ida heard the buzzing.

He gasped at the faint, unfamiliar noise and glanced around, but nothing seemed out of the ordinary. Within moments, Kaminari, Ojiro, and Koji Koda had all popped out of their rooms to join Ida in the third-floor corridor.

"Were you all awake this whole time?" asked Ida.

"After hearing that story, I couldn't sleep a wink," admitted Ojiro with a pained smile.

"Seriously, though—what's that crazy noise?" said Kaminari. He and an equally terrified Koda scanned the hallway for the source of the sound but couldn't find a thing. The four boys glanced at each other warily.

Then, a small scream from below.

"Was that Mineta?" asked Kaminari.

"Let's check!" said Ida with a nod.

They raced down to the second floor to find a trembling Mineta clinging to Midoriya's leg. Yuga Aoyama and Tokoyami stood nearby, looking drained.

"What happened?" asked Ida.

"Sh-she called my name again!" said Mineta.

"I heard it too. First a knock on Mineta's door, then a voice..." added Midoriya, and Tokoyami and Aoyama corroborated his account. They all seemed more than serious enough to give Ida pause.

"What on earth is behind all this...?" he wondered.

That night, the entire class heard the buzzing.

U.A.

"A noise. Really?"

Shota Aizawa did nothing to hide the doubt in his voice, though his entire class looked as gloomy as the overcast sky. The weather forecast was calling for a storm that night, and stronger and stronger winds were already whipping through the trees outside.

The kids had all slept terribly and had been unable to focus in classes, earning Aizawa's quiet wrath during the final homeroom of the day. The teacher was used to one or two slackers, but the issue was widespread enough to make him demand an explanation.

"You can't possibly believe in something so irrational as the paranormal, though," he said, visibly annoyed.

"W-we don't, necessarily," said Yaoyorozu, her voice cracking. "But after a series of inexplicable events, we can't help but be shaken..." The six girls of 1-A had also heard the buzzing and had spent the night huddled with their respective floor mates.

Ida shot his hand up and stood.

"Sensei! This is a real predicament! Some anomaly is afflicting our living quarters, and if this keeps up,

I'm afraid it will affect our academic performance! I believe we ought to ascertain the cause and resolve the matter posthaste!"

"I-I can't take it anymore! No way I'm getting a wink of sleep when that ghost keeps calling my name! I mean, if she wanted to join me for cuddles... Wait, no, she'd probably just murder me in bed! But then again, if this ghost wanted to show up naked... Nope, even then, no curses for me! No thanks!" said Mineta, clutching his face as he considered the erotic potential of a spectral curse.

"Paranormal happenings... I remember hearing about that here at U.A." said Aizawa, recalling something.

The whole class stared, wide eyed, and Ashido blurted out, "Seriously?"

"One of the 'Seven Mysteries of U.A.,' yeah..." said Aizawa, as calmly as ever. "They say that the ghost of an alum who couldn't make it as a hero haunts the campus, cursing anyone who spots it. Especially in the woods behind the main building, which is... Oh. Right where they built the dorms, actually."

The class sat still for a beat before erupting in pandemonium.

"And now that ghost is haunting our new home!"

"Nooo!"

"Heights Alliance is, like, totally haunted!"

The class was prone to laughing off most things, but the terror of a ghostly haunting was too much for the kids' psyches. Aizawa sighed, regretting his addition of fuel to the fire.

"Listen..." he started.

"If the whole building's haunted, we've got nowhere to run!"

"S-salt! We need salt to purify the place! Wait, crud, all we've got is that *gomashio* salt full of sesame seeds!"

"Do y'think the ghost will come after me even though I'm invisible? Please say no, please say no," shrieked Hagakure.

Since he did feel responsible for riling up the class even further, Aizawa tried using kid gloves to calm everyone down. But alas, they forced him in the end to resort to one of his usual sharp rebukes.

"Enough already!"

With an almost Pavlovian response, the class registered Aizawa's low voice as it penetrated the hubbub—the voice that meant serious business. They

fought to contain their fear and, though still trembling, fell silent. Aizawa gave them a conciliatory sigh and decided to throw them a bone.

"If this disturbance is really such a problem, I'll drop by tonight to check it out. That's the rational approach, especially since it'll be storming tonight. So be sure to be in your rooms when I come around to do the roll call."

"Th-thank you, Sensei!"

They could feel the love from their teacher, even if he was as blunt about it as ever.

U/A

The rain began that evening, and it was coming down in sheets by nightfall. Whipping winds rattled the windows of the sturdy Heights Alliance building. Construction of the dorm building had taken only three days, so the students hoped it would stand up to nature's fury.

Aizawa arrived for his inspection and surveyed the first floor. Outside the windows, the storm buffeted the trees violently. They might not last the night, Aizawa thought, and he feared for the streetlamps by the front door as well.

There was a sudden low rumbling in the distance and a flash of lightning across the dark sky. A storm of this magnitude could cause a blackout, so Aizawa wanted to be prepared for the worst. He double-checked the location of the breaker switch (in case the backup generators failed), flashlights, and other emergency supplies.

The real problem…will be the kids themselves.

Aizawa scowled, remembering the childish uproar in the classroom earlier. If they experienced a blackout on tonight of all nights… Just imagining it practically gave him a headache. The mysterious noise in the night couldn't be overlooked, though; passing it off as a mass hallucination would be irrational indeed.

"So what's making this noise…?" muttered Aizawa to himself as he glanced around the first floor. He sensed something nearby and detected a slight mechanical buzzing, barely audible amid the rain, the creaking trees, and the rattling windows.

What is that…?

With bated breath, he searched the first floor, attempting to track down the source of the noise. Knowing that this was likely what the kids had heard somehow allowed Aizawa to focus his senses even more. It wasn't coming from any one direction; it was on the move.

Something alive...? Wait, no. Oh, you've got to be kidding me...

Aizawa stared in surprise at the source, which he discovered in the dining area.

UA

As the second bolt of lightning struck the earth, Ida was paying a visit to Mineta's room, accompanied by Todoroki, Sato, and Sero. The class president had found it odd when their teacher hadn't shown up for the roll call at the appointed time, so he'd taken it upon himself to ask around.

"Nope. No Aizawa here. Maybe he started up top?" said Mineta, who'd been lying awake in terror of receiving a ghostly visitor again. Fifth-floor resident Sato said, "Nope. He didn't show."

"Hey, guys…" said a troubled Midoriya, appearing from one end of the corridor. "Kinda weird that Aizawa Sensei hasn't come by, like he promised…"

"P-pointing it out just makes it scarier, Midoriya! When it could be another 'rational deception,' like he's always doing!" said Mineta.

"Let's find Sensei," said Ida, as he and his posse arrived on the first floor.

"Craaazy weather out there, huh?" said Sero, glancing out the window at the pounding rain.

"Perhaps Sensei is preparing for the worst outcome of this extreme weather event? As U.A. students, we must ensure we're ready to take action as well!" added Ida.

Midoriya gasped.

"Wait! Look, over there… Is that Aizawa Sensei…?"

Their teacher lay on the floor near the dining table.

UA

"How on earth did this happen?" asked Yaoyorozu with a grave shake of her head.

Aizawa was still out cold, though at least the kids

had carried him to the sofa. Given the dire situation, the entire class was now gathered in the common area.

"D-don't tell me he's got a blond hair on his neck…" said Kaminari, almost too scared to look. "Ack! He does! Oh wait. That's just one of my hairs."

"Don't freaking joke about that, dunce-face!" roared Bakugo—just like always—but a trained ear might've detected a slight stiffness to his voice.

"He got whammied by the curse, for sure!" cried Mineta. "I mean, what else?"

"It could've been a villain attack. But they'd have to be a tough customer to knock out Aizawa Sensei!" said Ojiro. The rest of the frightened class kept freaking out about curses, ghosts, and villains.

"Calm yourselves, everyone!" shouted Ida, but his attempt to quiet his classmates went unheard through the din. Asui, however, found just the right moment to insert her levelheaded thoughts.

"Paranormal occurences aside, we should alert the other teachers about what happened to Aizawa Sensei."

This brought them to their senses.

"Well said, Tsuyu!" agreed Ida. "There should be a landline phone in Sensei's room, so—"

Ida was interrupted by crashing thunder, and an instant later, Heights Alliance went dark.

"Eek!"

"Just what we needed—a blackout..."

"R-restrain yourself, Dark Shadow!"

"Geez, Tokoyami! Don't release Dark Shadow now, in here!"

"Wahhh! Somebody save me!"

With the lights out, there was no telling who was who. Humans have always instinctively feared the dark, and talk of the paranormal and ghosts only triggered that latent, primal fear in the kids of class 1-A.

"Everyone! There's nothing to fear!" shouted Ida.

"Th-that's right, no cause for alarm, now!" said Yaoyorozu. She attempted to take action by using her "Creation" Quirk to produce a working flashlight, but before she could, something scurried across her feet.

"Ahhh!"

"Was that you, Momoyao? W-what happened?" asked Jiro.

"S-something is running about underfoot!" said Yaoyorozu, her voice shaking.

"Whaddaya mean, 'something'...? Eek! I felt it too!"

said Uraraka. Whatever it was, it was quick.

"I can't deal with any more somethings!" said Kaminari, almost in tears. The disturbance darted around the room, raising shrieks from more members of the class.

"We need some light!" commanded Ida. This was enough to snap Kaminari and Bakugo into action; they used their respective Quirks to illuminate the room for a brief moment, during which the class saw a flash of white jumping through the air before disappearing back into the darkness. Most students were too stunned to scream at first, but like the light, that silence didn't last either.

"W-w-w-what was thaaat?" said Hagakure.

"Definitely a ghost! That's what ghosts look like, right? Somebody back me up—I've never seen one before," said Kaminari, in full panic mode.

Even Todoroki was shaken, but at least now he knew Midoriya was nearby.

"M-Midoriya... Which is more effective against ghosts—ice or fire?"

"Huh? I can't say I've ever thought about that, but we think of ghosts as being cold, right? So maybe fire would work? But honestly, I'm not sure physical attacks have any effect on spirits! Since, by definition, they don't have corporeal bodies," said Midoriya, managing to provide a reasonable analysis despite being equally disturbed.

"Then what do we do...?" said Todoroki, sinking into despair.

"We're done for, guys!" screamed Mineta. "About to die by ghosts for sure! Dammit! I always wanted to die being crushed between some hot babes' bodies!"

The front door swung open, and the kids froze. Backlit by a flash of lightning, a figure with long blond hair stepped into the building. As the figure shuffled toward the group, drops of rainwater dripped from its hair onto the floor.

"Ugh... You kids..." said the apparition, raising its head toward them. Somebody screamed.

"The blond ghost!"

The class had already received plenty of training on how to counter villains, but none of those lessons had mentioned spectral opponents, so when they attacked the home invader in a panic, they didn't exactly hold back. Tokoyami's Dark Shadow flew ahead of the pack.

"This prey is mine!" it roared.

"Whoa… Hang on!" said the blond figure, but its voice was drowned out by the barrage of Quirk-powered attacks. The kids snapped out of it when they heard the figure fall to the floor. A moment later, the lights came back on, and Dark Shadow retreated back into Tokoyami with a yelp. Though the class was relieved to see clearly again, they didn't let their guards down just yet. A combination of explosions, ice crystals, fire, and acid had produced a cloud of smoke, and as it cleared, the defeated ghost came into view.

"Th-the ghost didn't disappear…?" said a shocked Mineta, whose own "Pop Off" balls were scattered here and there, stuck to the floor and walls. Still on high alert, he and the others crept toward the motionless figure. Between the stringy strands of blond hair, they spotted a short, manicured mustache. Though relatively slender, the body was much more than skin and bones.

"This ain't a lady. And that 'stache looks familiar…" said Ashido, peering at the supposed ghost's face. Jiro got a look from behind Ashido, gasped, and went pale.

"It's Present Mic Sensei!"

Shock and horror. Their boisterous English teacher's

hair was usually gelled to the nines and sticking straight up, so they hadn't recognized him with a flat, soaking-wet do.

"S-Sensei? Present Mic Sensei!" cried Uraraka, clearly worried.

Jiro used one of her "Earphone Jack" earlobes to check for a heartbeat.

"Phew. He's just knocked out."

"Perhaps," said Ida, "he came by to check on us during the blackout? Quite the reception we gave him..." The class president was feeling guilty.

"What's going on...?" came a familiar voice from behind.

The class spun around. Aizawa was standing, awoken by the clamor a moment ago. They ran to him, finally feeling a bit less panicked.

"We thought the blond ghost was here to murder us, so we attacked on sight!"

"Sensei, what knocked you unconscious? Was it a villain? Or a real ghost...?"

"Hang on, there really is that little white ghost running around the dorm!"

Like a conditioned reflex, they piped down and

straightened up after one more sharp "Enough" from Aizawa. First, he had them carry Present Mic away from the wet, windswept doorway. Then he started scanning the ceiling, moving around the space while the confused class followed behind instinctively.

"Hold on," said Jiro. "What about the buzzing noise?"

The class gasped, suddenly remembering that unsolved mystery.

"I figured it out," said Aizawa. Upon finding what he was looking for, he pointed to a spot on the ceiling and said, "Asui, see that tiny thing up there? Get it down."

"The black one? Okay, Sensei."

Asui's long, sticky tongue shot out and nabbed a black object too small to identify from afar. She handed over the buzzing device to her teacher.

"This is the source of your noise, and it's what knocked me out, indirectly."

"What? How?"

"I noticed it on the ceiling, but when I climbed on the table to get it down, I slipped on a kitchen rag that *somebody* had left out."

"Oops, that was me! Totally forgot to put it back when I remembered we had to be in our rooms!" said

Hagakure with a sheepish giggle.

Aizawa turned to the invisible girl with a glare that promised a good scolding but decided against it.

"Never mind that. Look."

He extended the hand that held the black object so the class could get a better look. As they stared, Yaoyorozu said, "Please use this," and passed around a magnifying glass she'd created on the spot. They realized it was a miniscule machine and that its motor was the source of the buzzing.

"Where'd this thing come from...?"

"I have a pretty good idea. You don't recognize it?" said Aizawa. He walked toward the newly affixed anti-peeping security panel at the door to the girls' bathing area and tossed the black machine toward it. The tiny device flew over to the panel and slotted into a hole, like an insect returning to its hive.

"Recharging... Recharging..." came a female voice.

Aizawa figured the most rational course of action would be to ask the inventor herself, so he called up Power Loader and asked his colleague to put Hatsume on the phone.

"Oh, that?" said Hatsume. "That'd be my supercute

add-on baby that goes on independent scouting missions at night! Since you've gotta live in the same space as that tenacious perv, what's his name... Mini... Minu...something? Doesn't matter! You know who I mean. Anyway, my baby is programmed to fly around at night to make sure that megaperv is in his room, where he belongs! Heh heh. Pretty handy, huh?"

The conversation ended abruptly and the phone went dead when Hatsume realized she had blueprints to get back to drawing.

"That meddling chick! Still, I'm sure glad it wasn't a haunting after all," said Mineta, feeling a combination of rage and relief.

"B-but what was the white ghost? You all saw it, right?" said Kaminari, just as the creature in question leaped into Koda's arms. Kaminari screamed before realizing it was none other than Koda's pet rabbit.

"I'm sorry, I must have forgotten to shut my door all the way..." said an embarrassed Koda, his large body in stark contrast with the small white animal he embraced. The rabbit had escaped his dorm room and run about in the chaos once the kids started panicking.

"Geez... And here I thought I'd spotted my first-ever real-life ghost," said Kaminari with a sigh.

With this last mystery solved, the kids' faces broke into smiles.

"All's well that ends well!"

"What, exactly, ended *well*?" said Aizawa in a low and menacing tone, prompting his class to gulp and notice the state of their common area. The wrecked entryway looked as if a bomb had gone off near the door, whose glass had been shattered and blown outside, allowing the wind and rain to pour and gush in.

"You barely just moved in, and already… Ugh. And ghost stories are to blame for all this? How could you let yourselves go to pieces over fairy tales?"

With his black hair whipped by the wind and his cold, red glare, Aizawa resembled a demon straight out of one of their tales. His class stood at rapt attention, experiencing a new type of fear.

"I want apology essays from each of you, by tomorrow! And for the next few days, at least, it's lights-out at eight, sharp! And no more ghost stories! Got it?"

"Yes, Sensei!"

Hauntings and ghosts were scary, but one of Aizawa's bad moods? A much more rational fear.

Part 5
A Day in the Life of a Class President

Tenya Ida's eyes popped open at the sound of a bird chirping outside his window. The sight of his dimly lit ceiling signaled the start of his day. He checked the alarm clock beside his pillow; it was set to go off in five minutes.

I might as well get up.

Ida turned off the alarm, stretched a bit, and got out of bed. After fixing the rumpled blanket, he proceeded with his daily routine by opening the curtains, which scared away the chirping bird on the veranda.

"I'm sorry, little one," he said as he opened the window.

The morning view of U.A.'s campus spread before him was quickly becoming a familiar one, but it was always bracing to behold. A deep breath of the still-chilly air was just the thing to invigorate Ida for the day ahead. No time to dawdle, though. Ida shut the window, did his business in his en suite bathroom, and left his dorm room. He carried with him his toothbrush, his towel, and everything else he'd need at the sink in the boys' changing room, which was attached to the bathing area down on the first floor.

"Again? Really...?" said Ida to himself, scowling at the state of the changing room. The baskets meant for holding bathers' clothes were scattered about, and the tissue box and other provisions were out of place. Somebody had even left his toothbrush behind.

"Of all the..." sighed Ida, as he straightened up the room and placed the forgotten toothbrush in a prominent spot by the sinks. It wasn't so messy that one couldn't traverse the room; in fact, one might expect a changing room shared by fourteen boys to be much, much worse. But Ida was the word *serious* in human form, so he most certainly classified it as a mess.

A living space in disarray begets minds in disarray. They must learn to keep things tidier...

He had scolded his classmates about this plenty

of times since they'd moved into the dorms, but the lesson never stuck. It ground Ida's gears. He faced the mirror and brushed his teeth as he pondered a new approach to the topic.

"Good morning, Shoji, Koda," said Ida, noticing the pair come into the changing room.

"You're up early again today, President," replied Mezo Shoji, who also stuck to a fairly regimented schedule. Behind him, a tired-looking Koji Koda gave a slight bow of acknowledgement. This was far from the first time Ida had bumped into these fellow early risers at this hour.

"Ah, do either of you happen to know who left this toothbrush behind?" asked Ida.

The two boys squinted at the toothbrush in his outstretched hand.

"Kaminari, maybe. I think his is that color," said Shoji.

"Very well. Thank you, Shoji. I'll have to rouse our forgetful classmate and ask him about it."

Ida left the changing room and bumped into Mashirao Ojiro on the third floor. The latter was yawning as he left his room with towel in hand and tail fur full of cowlicks.

"Good morning, Ojiro."

"Good morning…"

Back in his room, Ida changed into his school uniform and placed his pajamas—neatly folded—into the laundry basket. He checked to make sure his window was locked, closed the curtains, and picked up his schoolbag—already full of the books and supplies he would need for the day's classes.

On his way to the elevator, he stopped at Denki Kaminari's room and knocked on the door.

"Kaminari! Are you awake? If not, perhaps you ought to be!"

A moment passed, and then some shuffling sounds came from within.

"Mornin'…" said Kaminari as he opened the door. Ida had grown concerned about Kaminari's tendency toward procrastination, so he'd been making an effort to wake his floor mate on mornings like this one.

"Good morning indeed, Kaminari! Did you happen to forget your toothbrush by the sinks?"

"*Yawwwn*… Huh? Oh. Maybe?"

"Well, I left it where you can't miss it. Be more mindful next time! See you in class, then."

Kaminari blinked lazily—still half-asleep—said, "Yayyy..." and nodded.

With that task out of the way, Ida made for the dining area on the first floor. The breakfast available (with both Japanese and Western options) was prepared early in the morning by the school's head cook, Lunch Rush, and delivered to the dorms. Dinner was also carted over later in the day.

As Ida was selecting his miso soup, Shoji, Koda, Fumikage Tokoyami, Momo Yaoyorozu, and Kyoka Jiro all showed up for breakfast. After saying "Good morning," each picked out some food and took a seat at the table.

"*Yawwn*... So sleepy..." said Jiro.

"Me too..." said Yaoyorozu, also yawning.

"Did something disturb your sleep?" asked Ida, turning to the girls.

"Nuh-uh... But last night, we..." started Jiro.

"Last night? What happened last night?"

Ida's question seemed to startle them.

"L-last night...I was up quite late, simply absorbed in one of my books..." said Yaoyorozu.

"And I, uh... I was listening to music. Like I do..." said Jiro.

But Ida sensed something awkward about the girls' explanations. On his other side, Tokoyami cleared his throat loudly and squinted at Ida's breakfast.

"I see you opt for a traditional Japanese breakfast, President."

"Quite right, Tokoyami. I'm grateful to Lunch Rush Sensei for providing us with such wonderful rice every morning!"

Ida had been taken off guard by the sudden pivot, but he assumed that Tokoyami must be equally enthusiastic about their surprisingly tasty school food. He finished every last grain of rice in his bowl, thanked the powers that be for the meal, and said, "See you all in class."

As he exited Heights Alliance, the gleaming tower that was his destination came into view, with the verdant grounds and blue sky reflecting off its polished glass surfaces. The main U.A. High building beckoned, inspiring Ida to pick up his pace.

He was grateful that the implementation of the dorm system had shortened his commute. It wasn't that Ida hadn't made good use of the original travel time from his family home—that too had been a valuable

opportunity to study or be alone with his thoughts—but having the school a stone's throw away meant more energy to devote to worthier tasks.

As Aizawa was prone to pointing out, time didn't grow on trees, so every minute of every day ought to be meaningful in some way.

U.A.

Ida arrived in the classroom within minutes, and what he saw revived the same frown from earlier in the changing room. Many of his classmates' chairs were out of place, despite his constant chiding about this very point.

Sloppy chairs lead to sloppy attitudes, so we must treat school property with greater respect.

Katsuki Bakugo's was always the worst.

"Of all the..." said Ida for the second time that day.

After slotting the chairs under their respective desks, Ida got the broom and dustpan from the closet and began sweeping. There was nothing like a clean classroom to allow students to focus on their studies, after all. Next, he wiped down the lectern with a damp rag so that their teachers could better focus on teaching. With his routine concluded, the class president surveyed the spick-and-span classroom and smiled.

Let us make today another meaningful day.

Ida took his own seat and began to review subject material in silence. After a solid night's sleep, early-morning studying was the perfect way to get the brain and body in gear for the rest of the day.

Before Ida knew it, it was three minutes to homeroom.

"Everyone sure is cutting it close..." he remarked. The entire class was usually present by this point, if not already in their seats. Ida tilted his head in concern, unsure why the classmates he'd run into at breakfast that morning weren't there already.

Another two minutes ticked by, and just as the class president was really starting to panic, he heard the approach of a minor stampede out in the hallway. Within seconds, the other nineteen members of class A barged into the classroom, practically tripping over each other.

"Phew, made it..." said Eijiro Kirishima, his shoulders sagging in relief.

"A full sprint this early in the day? Not fun at all," added Mina Ashido.

"What on earth were you all up to? Are you aware that homeroom is about to begin?" asked the concerned Ida, his arms wildly swinging side to side. His classmates froze and then broke into a series of awkward *Umm*'s and *Well, y'know*'s.

"Actually, y'see..." started Ochaco Uraraka, facing Ida. "We ran into some big old C-words."

"C-word? Which C-word is that?"

"The creepy-crawly buggers that show up in the kitchen sometime. Those you-know-whats..."

"Ah! You mean *Periplaneta japonica*, or the common cockroa—"

"Don't say it!" shot back Uraraka with a distinctly non-Uraraka expression. "Wouldn't want to jinx it and summon another one, especially after we just got done exterminating!"

The intensity of her stare and tone made Ida flinch, but he recovered and clamped his hands down on his friend's shoulders.

"I apologize that I wasn't there to assist! That sounds like quite the ordeal!"

This made the others breathe a collective sigh of relief. As they took their seats, Izuku Midoriya and Shoto Todoroki greeted Ida wearily.

"Good morning, Ida."

"Hey."

"And good morning to you as well, Midoriya, Todoroki. It's a bit early to be looking so exhausted, no?"

"Exhausted? Us? Nah... We're not tired, right, Todoroki?"

"Guess not."

As Ida's two friends made for their seats, he couldn't help but feel that something was amiss. Before Ida could voice his concern, he turned around and caught notice of Uraraka's hair.

"Why, Uraraka! I've never known you to tolerate cowlicks."

"Huh? Dang, really? I must not've slept well, staying up so late," she said as she hastily smoothed down her hair with her hands. Like the hair, this comment caught Ida's attention, since Yaoyorozu and Jiro had also mentioned having late nights.

"What kept you up, may I ask?" said Ida.

"I was just—"

But before she could finish, Uraraka clamped her own hands over her mouth.

"Uraraka?"

"N-nothing! No special reason. Just didn't sleep well, I guess!"

Right on cue, Aizawa strolled through the door, prompting the kids to snap into their seats. A number of strange things were weighing on Ida's mind, but those concerns would have to come later. First period would start immediately after homeroom, and these lessons demanded focus.

UA

The first four periods of the day flew by.

At lunchtime, Ida made his way to Lunch Rush's Cafeteria with Midoriya and Todoroki, just like always, and as per usual, the large space was packed with students—from all grade levels and courses of study— hoping to fill their bellies at a reasonable cost. The trio of 1-A boys followed the crowd and got in line.

"Lunch Rush Sensei must be busier than ever since the dorms were built," said Ida.

"He's making a whole lot more than just lunch now," added Todoroki, which made Midoriya think.

"I wonder if he'll revise his hero name? To 'Three-Squares Rush' or something?"

"No, I feel he ought to specifically reference breakfast, lunch, and dinner. 'B.L.D. Rush,' perhaps?" offered Ida.

"Ooh, 'B.L.D.' sounds like the name of some new sandwich," said Midoriya.

"Pretty sure you can't just change your hero name at the drop of a hat," said Todoroki.

As the boys chatted, a trio of third-year students ahead of them in line—U.A.'s so-called Big Three—were having another conversation.

"Ugh... Why does this place always have to be so crowded? Can't take it... Need to get outta here. Maybe I'll take my lunch and eat in the corner of the classroom..." whined Tamaki Amajiki, who at a glance seemed far too timid to be considered one of U.A.'s top three hero hopefuls.

"You've been like this since we were first-years!" said

Nejire Hado, in her usual practical way. "Kinda weird how you still haven't adapted, huh! Huh! Hey, Togata, didja decide what to get yet? Me, I've been craving cold *chuka* noodles all day! Did I mention that earlier?"

"I'm going for ramen, with extra *chashu* pork! And I'll save a piece for you, Tamaki!" said Mirio Togata, all smiles and charm.

"Thanks..." muttered Amajiki gratefully. "Pork, sure... That'll give me a stronger sniffer for today, I guess."

"So what're you getting, Amajiki? Huh? Huh? It's your turn to order! Didn'tcha notice?" said Hado.

"Ah... Um... What to get, what to get..."

"How about *vongole*, Tamaki? You like clams, right?" suggested Togata.

"Okay. Why not..."

The Big Three placed their orders, got their food, and strolled past the first-year trio. Though they didn't know it at the time, it wouldn't be long before class 1-A would get a guest presentation on work studies from the Big Three themselves.

When it was their turn to order, each of the boys picked his favorite dish: Ida got beef stew (with a glass of orange juice on the side), Midoriya chose the *katsudon* pork bowl, and Todoroki went for soba noodles served on a wickerwork tray. They found a table and were soon approached by Rikido Sato.

"Mind if I sit here too?" asked Sato.

"Of course n—"

"Go ahead! We sure don't mind, right, Ida?" said Midoriya, interrupting Ida a bit too eagerly. Sato took a seat opposite the trio.

As he ate his lunch, Ida found himself reflecting on the events of the morning.

"Ah, a question, friends!" he said with a start. "How might I convince our fellow male classmates to keep the changing room tidier? When I went to freshen up this morning, I found the room in a state of disarray."

"That bad, huh?" asked Sato.

Ida nodded. "Yes, the baskets were askew, and I feel the issue could be solved if we were all just a bit more mindful…"

"Hmm, maybe put up a sign? Like a friendly reminder?" offered Midoriya.

"Or stick magnets on the floor," suggested Todoroki.

"So the baskets could snap right back into position every time."

They went back and forth for a minute until Sato interrupted.

"B-by the way, is there anything you can't eat, Ida...?"

"Foods I dislike? No, I can't say I'm all that picky."

"Any food allergies, then?"

"No, none that I know of."

"Great! Glad to hear it!" said Sato with a wide, satisfied grin that caused Ida to beam in response.

"Thank you for asking, though! Is there any reason in particular you'd need to know such a thing?"

At Ida's question, both Midoriya and Sato flinched. Ida found this odd, but before he could ponder their reaction, Todoroki finished the soba noodles he was slurping and raised his head.

"Cuz it's your—"

"Todoroki!" yelped Midoriya, who leaped out of his seat to clamp his hands over his friend's mouth. Midoriya's momentum threatened to send them both toppling to the ground, but Ida was quick enough to extend an arm and keep them upright.

"What ever is the matter, Midoriya?"

"N-nothing, really! I mean, uh, I noticed a scallion stuck to the corner of his mouth... Right, Todoroki?"

"Oops... Sorry. I was so caught up in my soba I got careless," said Todoroki.

"Careless? How do you mean?" asked Ida.

"He didn't mean a thing! *Right*, Todoroki...?"

"Right... I mean, the scallion. On my face. So careless."

Something was off about the entire exchange, and Ida was once again reminded of the strange happenings throughout the day. Firstly, it wasn't like Yaoyorozu, Jiro, and Uraraka to stay up particularly late. Ida thought back and realized that Tsuyu Asui, Mina Ashido, and Toru Hagakure had also been yawning like mad during the breaks between class periods. And now Midoriya and Todoroki's clumsy attempt to cover up *something*. They were the types to wear their emotions on their sleeves, yet they insisted that nothing was the matter. It was also bizarre how late all nineteen of Ida's classmates had arrived in the classroom.

Did I perhaps do something to offend without realizing it?

In searching for an explanation for the recent changes in his classmates, that was Ida's first thought. He decided that the next word Todoroki had been about to utter after "Cuz it's your—" was "fault." That was hardly a logical follow-up to Ida asking why Sato wanted to know about allergies, but Ida's distress over these disturbing events led him to that self-deprecating conclusion all the same.

So the class has decided to lie to me, shun me, ostracize me... But why? What on earth did I do to deserve such treatment?

Ida searched his memories, and it suddenly seemed obvious.

He was constantly warning Bakugo not to open doors with his feet. He had scolded Yuga Aoyama for staring into the mirror at length after bathing. He had told off Minoru Mineta for bringing adult magazines into the common area. He had lectured the boys about practicing their backstroke in the communal bath. He had chided them for getting Dark Shadow riled up at bath time, which resulted in foamy bubbles everywhere. And when Kaminari had decided to cover himself in body soap and slide around like a hockey puck, Ida had forbidden that particular antic from going forward.

Then there was that other time, when I...

The list was endless. His complaint about the messy changing room just moments ago, too, had probably come off as needless nagging. Suddenly, Ida's favorite beef stew wasn't hitting the spot anymore.

"Ida? Everything okay?"

Ida's abrupt silence hadn't escaped Midoriya's notice.

"Yes, of course. I'm perfectly fine!" said Ida. He could tell that the concern on his friend's face was genuine, at least. As he finished his lunch, he gave the predicament a bit more thought.

It's not as though I have proof, so it's shameful of me to doubt my friends. Yes, I must be reading into things too much.

But for the rest of the day, his classmates kept giving him the cold shoulder and keeping their interactions with Ida bizarrely brief, so by the time afternoon classes were over, his nagging doubt had turned to solid conviction. After all, when had the kids of class 1-A ever held back from speaking their minds, besides the times when Aizawa was lecturing them? The departure from the norm was even more striking once they got back to the dorm building—especially when, after an awkwardly silent dinner, they all left their seats simultaneously and with unusual efficiency.

Something is definitely odd, here...

Desperate to get to the bottom of the mystery, Ida decided to take his bath ahead of his usual schedule, since the boys might be more willing to open up in a space where they were already so exposed, physically. When Ida arrived in the changing room, he realized most of them were already bathing. Their respective bath times usually didn't overlap to this extent. As Ida approached the closed door to the bath, he heard the animated conversation within.

"This part's gotta be Midoriya or Todoroki."

"Oh, uh-huh. Makes sense."

"That's a big responsibility."

Ida could make out Kirishima's voice, and then Midoriya's and Todoroki's responses.

They're being entrusted with a task of some importance, then...?

The class president found his resolve and reached for the sliding door, but as he stepped into the room, Kaminari blurted out something not meant for Ida's ears.

"Let's just hope Ida decides to hole up in his room early tonight."

"Ack!" said Midoriya, noticing Ida standing in the doorway.

The boys flinched, and Kaminari—looking like a kid caught with his hand in the cookie jar—sank down into the water until half his face was submerged. The lively conversation died, giving way to uneasy silence.

This is somehow about me, as I thought.

"It would seem you're all speaking about me?" said Ida, screwing up his courage.

"S-say what? You? Nah! Whoops... Fingers are getting all pruney! Must've been in the bath too long!" stammered Kaminari.

"W-what he said!" added Midoriya. "Later, Ida."

With that, the boys practically charged out of the bath, leaving Ida all by his lonesome in the steamy room. He washed himself in silence at a stall before

stepping into the bath proper for a soak. He'd made a habit of always bathing with at least one other person since moving into Heights Alliance, so now, alone in the wide communal tub, he felt lost at sea, his mind adrift. With one last splash of water to the face, Ida stood and left.

[UA]

"Midoriya, might I speak to you in my room for a moment?" said Ida, singling out his friend from the group in the common area.

"Huh? Oh, sure!"

Midoriya seemed ill at ease on the trip up to the third floor.

"This shouldn't take too long—I know you have some business to conduct with Todoroki."

"Eh? Why would you think that?"

"Apologies, but I overheard the conversation in the bath, earlier."

"Oh, that? Nothing you have to worry about!"

Midoriya's obvious panic made Ida frown, since this

was far from the first time he'd heard "It's nothing" and "Don't worry" that day. Not to mention, there was no better sign that something was indeed something than the insistent claim that something was nothing.

"I need you to be honest with me, Midoriya, as my friend. Have I done something to make you and the others dislike me?"

Midoriya's eyes grew wide at Ida's grave concern.

"I couldn't help but notice," continued Ida, "how oddly you've all been acting, and I need to know why so that I may take steps to improve. So please, tell m—"

"That's not it! Not at all!"

"But..."

"I promise, that's not the case!"

Hearing this from Midoriya in no uncertain terms gave Ida some relief, but then his friend glanced at the clock on the wall, gasped, and panicked.

"You're overthinking things, Ida. Are you getting enough sleep, buddy? That must be it! Better call it a night!"

Ida looked at the clock; it was far too early for bed.

"No, I don't feel tired in the least..."

"Doesn't matter! Just lie down, and you'll get

sleepy before you know it! C'mon, just...lie...down...
already!"

Midoriya practically shoved Ida's head onto the
pillow and covered him with the blanket, before
saying a quick "Good night," flipping the light switch,
and dashing out of the room.

U.A.

With eyes shut, Ida attempted to follow his friend's
orders, but he simply wasn't feeling sleepy.

"Aha!"

His eyes flashed open as he made the connection
between Midoriya's strange behavior and what he'd
overheard Kaminari saying in the bath.

They really wanted to be rid of me that badly...?

Since starting his high school career at U.A., Ida
had come to know his quirky classmates, learned more
about the areas in which he needed improvement, and
found some friends he respected. He was constantly
striving to make every day a meaningful one, especially
since being elected class president. It was Ida's duty

to lead the class to a better tomorrow. He couldn't understand why they would suddenly ostracize him, but he guessed that perhaps they were fed up with his strict, faultfinding ways.

"I promise, that's not the case!"

Midoriya's declaration echoed in Ida's mind. Those heartfelt words from a true friend.

I can't take this anymore.

Ida sprang out of bed and left his room. Even if his classmates were shunning him, he was still fond of them—warts and all—especially given everything they'd overcome together so far. No, he could never bring himself to resent them, and if there was to be any hope of tackling the challenges to come, he had to confront them now.

Ida boarded the elevator, and as he watched the floor display tick down, he felt an odd combination of resolve and nerves deep in his gut. Upon arriving on the first floor, the doors opened to reveal an unlikely obstacle.

"Huhh?" said Bakugo, glaring at Ida suspiciously, presumably on his way up to his room.

But Bakugo made no effort to board the elevator. He only stood there staring, as if deep in thought.

"I would like to get out, Bakugo," said Ida, but even this polite comment didn't make the boy budge, so he decided to spell it out.

"It's customary, Bakugo, for people to step off the elevator before others get on, so that they don't need to bump past each other in the cramped space. So if you wouldn't mind—"

But Ida caught himself. There he'd gone again, lecturing a classmate.

He could hear the others' cheery voices over in the common area.

"Too cool! I'd think you bought it at the store, if I didn't know better!"

"Looks delish! Great job as always, Sato!"

It sounds as though they're about to enjoy one of Sato's cakes or other confectionary creations...?

At the sound of this get-together, the steely resolve Ida had found in the elevator began to melt away. He stood there in silence as the elevator doors started to close, but at the last second, Bakugo pried the doors back open, stepped in, and jabbed the "Close Door" button.

"I'm actually getting out, Bakugo. As I previously explained..."

"What floor's your room on?"

"Oh, have you forgotten? I reside on the third floor."

Bakugo clucked his tongue in annoyance before pressing "3" and then "4," for his own room. As the elevator started to move, he turned to Ida.

"Don't you dare go back down there and interfere, four-eyes. Go back to your room and stick your nose in a book, or whatever crap you do to pass the time."

Ida couldn't figure out how to respond during the brief elevator ride, so when they reached the third floor, he stepped out slowly, without a word. On the trip back to his room, he reflected on the festivities he'd heard on the first floor as well as Bakugo's warning. Just the thought of the class going silent at Ida's arrival—as the boys had in the bath—made every step he took feel leaden and painful. Of course he'd never wanted to "interfere" with anyone's fun.

As Ida stepped into his room, his cell phone rang on his desk. Caller ID told him it was his mother.

"Hello, Mother."

"Tenya! How are things? Getting used to life in the dormitory?"

"Yes. I suppose," said Ida, after a pause. His mother picked up on his hesitation and responded quietly.

"Well… You haven't had too long to adjust yet, of course."

Ida knew that he'd be unable to hide his angst if the conversation went on, and the last thing he wanted to do was worry his mother, so he changed the subject.

"What's he talking about now?" came another voice from the phone. Ida pondered for a moment and gasped.

"Is Tensei there? Is he okay?"

"Your brother is just fine. Making lots of progress in his recovery, even," replied his mother.

Ida's relief didn't last long, because the light in his room suddenly blinked off.

"Anyhow, since today is your b—"

"Apologies, Mother, but we seem to be experiencing a blackout! Is everything okay on your end?"

"Huh? Yes, we're all right."

"I'm sorry, but I'll have to call you back!"

Ida hung up and felt his way out of the dark room. The lights in the corridor were out too.

Another blackout, really...? It's not storming like it was the other day... In any case, I had better make sure the others are safe!

Despite the apparent power outage, the elevator was still running. Perhaps the backup generator had kicked in, Ida thought as he pressed the button for the first floor. For a moment, his feet felt as leaden as they had earlier, but he quickly shook off the dark thoughts.

This is a potential emergency, so personal feelings must be set aside. I am the president of class A, after all.

The first floor was also pitch-black and bathed in complete silence.

I expected they would all still be here... Did they somehow steal away to their rooms in the meantime?

Ida didn't have much time to think about it, because Uraraka's piercing scream echoed from the common area.

"Eek!"

"Uraraka? What's the matter?"

"S-save me, Ida! Quick! This way!"

"I'll be there in a jiffy! Hang in there!" shouted Ida as he relied on touch and memory to dash across the space.

A villain attack, perhaps? What would be the best

way to counter an invasion in here…? No, the top priority is rescuing Uraraka!

Ida's leg brushed against the couch as he rushed to the source of his friend's screams.

"Where are you, Uraraka?"

"Right here," said Uraraka in her usual chipper voice, just as the lights popped back on.

"You're all here?" gasped Ida. The entire class—except Bakugo and Sato—was gathered before his eyes. Behind them, colorful balloons and handmade paper flowers decorated one corner of the common area. Hanging from the window nearby was a banner whose message they now shouted in unison.

"Happy birthday, Ida!"

They all simultaneously pulled the cords on the party poppers they held. All except a flustered Todoroki, who—late to the proverbial party—punctuated the chorus of pops with a delayed one of his own.

Multicolored confetti filled the air, and Ida stood stunned.

"My birthday…?" he stammered. "I had completely forgotten…"

That must have been why Mother was calling…

The class ran up to Ida, surrounding him.

"We really pulled off the surprise, huh!" said a giggling Uraraka.

"What a nerve-racking day, though. Especially when we had to go over the plan just after Ida left for class. I was sure we would be tardy..." said Yaoyorozu, patting her chest to calm herself.

"So true," added Jiro with a grimace.

"We stayed up late making all these decorations, y'know!" said Ashido.

"Thank goodness we finished in time, ribbit," said Asui.

"And then we had to toss them all up at top speed while you were back in your room, Ida," said Ojiro.

Kaminari clapped his hands together in apology.

"Sorry, man! I know that must've come off real weird, back in the bath!"

"This'll probably be the only time we go all out, though," said Sero with a grin. "Like, a special way of saying thanks to the class president who never quits on us!"

Kirishima, meanwhile, scratched his head disappointedly.

"Real shame Bakugo couldn't stick around. Dude said he was getting sleepy and stormed off..."

Ida thought back on his bizarre interaction with Bakugo, who must've known about the party decorating going on just across the room. If Ida had walked in on that, the surprise would've been ruined.

Was Bakugo actually being...considerate?

Maybe considerate was going too far, but Ida felt like he'd seen a new side of his surliest classmate that day, and it brought a smile to his face.

"And hey, sorry about that weirdness in the cafeteria," said Midoriya. "I panicked when Todoroki started blabbing."

"Yeah. My bad," said Todoroki.

"I must admit, that was the point when I really became suspicious," said Ida, which made Midoriya feel even guiltier.

"Sorry I couldn't tell you the truth earlier, but..." Midoriya paused. "But I meant what I said, about how it wasn't what you were thinking! Of course we like you!"

Ida looked at the smiling faces that surrounded him, each of them thrilled that they'd pulled off the surprise party. Just knowing the awkward lengths they'd gone to all day to keep it under wraps filled Ida with a warm and fuzzy feeling.

"Hey, when's it gonna be time for the main event?" called a voice from the kitchen. The class turned to see Sato's face peeking from around the corner.

At Yaoyorozu's signal, they started singing "Happy Birthday," and that was Sato's cue to carry the platter with the cake over to Ida. The brilliant orange cake was topped with sixteen lit candles. The panel of chocolate in the middle said, "Happy birthday, President! Thank you for all that you do! —Class A."

"Now you get why I was asking about your preferences and allergies, yeah? Anyway, this thing's made with orange juice, just for you, Ida. Not even from concentrate!"

"It's...magnificent. Thank you," said Ida, clearly moved.

"You gotta blow out the candles quick, Ida!" said Uraraka.

"And think of a wish when you do," added Asui.

"A wish...?"

Urged on by the class, Ida took a deep breath.

"My wish...is to be a worthy president for the fine

members of class A!" he said, before blowing out the candles with a mighty breath.

"I said *think*, not *say out loud*, Ida."

"What good is my wish if I can't announce it to you all?"

This left the rest of them stumped, so Ida let loose with a hearty laugh.

"Never mind that! I would just ask that you keep putting up with me, going forward!"

Ida's smile was infectious, and as the faces around him beamed and grinned, he couldn't help but feel proud. He'd have to remember to give his mother a call back and tell her—now, with confidence—that while life in the dormitory had its ups and downs, every wonderful day spent with his friends was well worth it.

Part 6
I Am a Rabbit

My owner, Koji, did not shut the door properly this morning, and this was very much my doing. I ran about the room last night to delay his sleep, so when he awoke this morning later than usual, he was forced to dash out in a hurry. I feel somewhat guilty about this premeditated mischief, but an animal can hardly defy its natural instincts.

My name is Yuwai. I am the pet rabbit belonging to Koji, who is wont to call me "Little Yuwai."

Speaking in terms of maturity, one might liken me to a human thirty years of age, which is supposedly the prime of a human's life. Would you dare call a thirty-year-old man "Little Yuwai"? I should think not. However, Koji put much thought into my name, so I do not balk at it. Coming to terms with such things is the first step a pet must take toward accepting its lot in life.

Unremarkably enough, Koji and I first met in a pet shop.

I am possessed of a white coat and charmingly round eyes, but despite the pride I take in my handsome appearance, poor timing or perhaps some other unfortunate factors led to most of my cohort in the shop being sold off merrily before my eyes while I remained to languish. Though this left me understandably despondent and with my confidence shredded, I never quite abandoned all hope.

During this dreadful limbo, I learned all manner of information about humans from my fellow unsold pets, as well those who came to the shop for treatment at the attached veterinary clinic. I educated myself in this way to prepare for my potential future as a kept animal. Finally, Koji appeared once he had amassed enough currency in his pockets to afford my considerably reduced price. That

I owe him a great debt for this kindness is a truth I will not forget for the rest of my days.

However, every pet has its pride. Had my new owner been the sort to snatch me up and squeeze me with little consideration for my feelings in the matter, I would no doubt have been inclined to resist in protest. To the good fortune of both parties, Koji was no such brute. With the utmost attention to my moods, he approached slowly, allowing us to grow closer on my terms. This, more than any other reason, is why I accept him as my owner.

What I did not expect was Koji's Quirk, "Anivoice"— an ability that allows him to impose his will upon nonhumans by simply speaking to us, though he rarely manipulates me in this manner. Only on occasions when I act incorrigibly, and once when he required that I swallow medicine for an upset stomach. Yes, through his respect for me, I learned quickly that Koji is the ideal owner. It is that trust that forms the basis of the relationship between pet and owner, so I am naturally inclined to respect him as well.

Though I am fundamentally a creature of the night, I have attempted to abandon my nocturnal ways in favor of diurnal ones so that I might better align my active hours with Koji's own schedule. In turn, my kindhearted owner endeavors to awaken in the morning as soon as I have.

Why, then, would I raise an intentional fuss last night, one might wonder? Because I glimpsed an opportunity to explore this unfamiliar structure that has become our new dwelling. The abrupt move from family home to dormitory left me initially out of sorts, but just as the humans believe that home is where one hangs one's proverbial hat, it is the fate of pets to reside wherever their owners may drift. There was talk of leaving me behind, but thankfully Koji decided to bring me along. Is there no end to my good fortune?

Perceptive as I am, I intuited that Koji was concerned about his prospects in this new environment. Hence, the necessity of my presence. He is, by nature, a kindly, quiet, and reclusive soul, lacking what other humans might consider an abundance of friends, which makes me a valuable companion indeed. Yes, he is at once owner, friend, and—given our respective ages—something of a dear little brother whom I find myself at all times concerned for. Perhaps you can understand now why I might hope to learn about this

fresh habitat we now share. It is also my nature and right, as a beast, to explore my territory. This is why I seized the opportunity to explore as I did.

IAI

The humans have left for school, and I am alone.

Despite my confidence on this point, I am nonetheless cautious as I slip past the doorframe and into the corridor, now flooded with light from the morning sun. My ears detect no sounds, no presences. Excellent. With relief in my heart, I traverse the corridor while sniffing with aplomb. The nearby window overlooks the courtyard below, and I lay eyes upon its lush, verdant lawn. A lawn I have seen from ground level as well, when Koji carries me to the first floor.

I swallow the saliva that fills my mouth in animalistic anticipation. Several factors have motivated my escape from the room, and that lawn is chief among them. In my dreams, I frolic through that grass and fill my belly with its crisp offerings. I even dig a small burrow, just for sport. Animals were made to thrive in nature, and a pet kept from such things is deprived indeed.

Fantasies of the lawn fill my mind, and I feel all reason slipping away. I must race to the first floor and ascertain whether or not a visit to the lawn is within my current power. As I hop toward the elevator, I pray that some careless child has left the front door ajar.

The layout of this building is not entirely clear to me, though Koji has carried me about enough to impart to me a vague understanding. My last foray beyond the confines of the room occurred several nights ago, when I emerged to find the children in a monstrous panic over an electrical failure.

Standing before the elevator doors, I leap and press the appropriate button. This astounding device allows one to travel between floors, and my observations have made me familiar with its methods of operation. The doors open within moments, and I hop inside. A jump to yet another button begins my descent, and I brace for the queer feeling of weightlessness that accompanies this journey. Suddenly, I hear a piercing noise that only grows when the doors open upon arrival at my destination.

What could make such a sound?

My instincts roar at me to flee, but I brace myself once more, reminding myself that this is an invaluable opportunity. I exit the elevator and crouch behind a series of objects, hidden from sight. The noise does not cease. Until I discover the source, an escape to the lawn is out of the question, so I creep in the direction of the disturbance.

The noise threatens to rend my ears apart. I recognize it now as the dreaded vacuum. Koji's mother used such a machine daily. I always despised the clamor, but keeping the house immaculate is by no means a contemptible desire, so I would dive under the blankets and endure it. Sadly, there are no blankets here.

I realize the sound is in fact two sounds. Two infernal vacuum cleaners? The very thought enrages me, but anger quickly gives way to dread. That there is a pair of the devices tells me there are no fewer than two humans in the building.

I endure the cacophony and peer around the corner. One vacuum sucks at the rug near the sofa, while the other is a few hops' distance away. The wielder of the first sports large eyes and a cheery countenance, while the other human's eyes are narrowed, his face pinched and somehow cruel. Midoriya and Bakugo are what the others call these two.

I recall a conversation from last night between Kaminari, Ida, and Ojiro, who share the third floor with my Koji. They were discussing these two boys.

"Y'think those two are gonna survive, being cooped up here together?"

This was said by Kaminari, whose attitude in all matters trends toward flippant. Unlike Koji, he is a gregarious human who often chooses, of his own free will, to speak to the others.

"You fear they might fight again, Kaminari?" said Ida. "I would hope they've learned their lesson, especially considering their temporary house arrest."

Ida sports a second pair of eyes, fashioned from glass. This dutiful human is often concerned for Koji's well-being, and he is fond of stating that, as class president, it is his responsibility to hold the class together, so to speak.

"They survived today, at least," said Ojiro.

Ojiro is neither as withdrawn as Koji, nor as aggressively outgoing as Kaminari; he achieves something of a happy medium. He boasts a magnificent tail, so I have to imagine that his character is just as impressive. I wish, someday, to confirm this hypothesis by sniffing that exquisite specimen of a tail.

"Yeah, but it's only been one day, and they gotta play nice for two more. Plenty of time for them to start brawling again. Don'tcha think, Koda?"

"I-I guess so..."

Yes, Kaminari was kind enough to include Koji in the conversation. I do wish Koji would insert himself more proactively, but I cannot fault him for his nature.

In any case, despite being privy to this discussion, the fact that Midoriya and Bakugo are heretofore confined to the building has somehow slipped my mind in my excitement. From what I could divine, the two boys snuck out from their rooms two nights ago and engaged in violent battle, leading to the current punishment. They were friends in childhood, though one would not know it from observing them at this age.

I am of the opinion that males of a species are entitled to a bit of roughhousing. I honestly doubt that Koji could even spell the word *fight*, and I fear that he would suffer astounding defeat should he be confronted with conflict. Battles between male rabbits are matters of life and death, and though I have never been forced to stomp the life from an enemy in mortal combat, I feel confident that I would do what is necessary to survive.

Matters are hardly so simple for humans, it seems. With the other children gone for the day, a fight between these two could very well turn deadly. While a rabbit killed in battle accepts his fate and returns to the earth, a slain human would create an uproar. Such an incident could very well cause trouble for Koji, given his proximity to the hypothetical victor and victim. I do not relish the thought.

"Ah?"

Hmm? I raise my head and lock eyes with Bakugo. Drat. I failed to notice when his vacuum ceased its racket.

"Why's this thing down here...?"

"What's going on, Kacchan? Oh! It's Little Yuwai!"

Now Midoriya has spotted me too. Curses. What am I to do…?

"Who the hell's 'Little Yuwai'?"

Bakugo's cheeky expression and tone are clearly mocking. Midoriya hurries to explain.

"That's the bunny's name."

"Tch. Who cares what it's called. It's that rocky guy's pet, yeah?"

"I guess Koda forgot to shut his door this morning? We'd better catch the little guy. Heeere, Yuwai…"

Midoriya approaches slowly as he beckons, but I maintain my distance.

"You're okay—just come to me now."

What sort of fool would willingly leap into his would-be captor's arms? No, I choose to edge even farther away from the boy.

"Just leave it. It's not like that thing can get outside."

"No way. Koda said that bunnies have fragile bones. What if Yuwai ran off and got hurt where we couldn't find him?"

"Then the idiot who forgot to shut his door is responsible."

I react to these words with a twitch. I caused Koji to

leave the door ajar, so I will not tolerate Bakugo's insults toward my owner. With hatred for this new enemy in my heart, I stamp the floor with my hind legs in defiance.

"The hell?" says Bakugo, appearing puzzled.

"I think he's mad...?" suggests Midoriya, tilting his head.

The latter is correct.

"The furball thinks it's tough, does it?"

This child hasn't the years behind him to speak of me this way. I unleash another stamp in Bakugo's direction. He grows visibly vexed, and a concerned Midoriya attempts to persuade him.

"We should really try to catch him. If something awful happens while we're on lockdown, who knows how angry Aizawa Sensei might get..."

"Tch. Like we didn't have enough work to do already."

The words have barely left Bakugo's lips before he has kicked off the ground and closed the distance between us. I flee in primal panic. Behind me, I hear him utter "Huh?"—plainly perplexed by my speed. Even in folklore, we rabbits are known for being fleet of foot, so you would do well not to underestimate me,

boy. Foolishly, I turn my head in hopes of spying a look of anguish upon Bakugo's face.

"Not in here, Kacchan!"

"Too slow, furball!"

Bakugo is producing explosions from his palms and is now flying toward me at ludicrous speed. How on earth...? Ah. His Quirk ability, of course. My body seizes up. Though I am ashamed to admit it, I am gripped by fear. The sound and scent of the explosions instill instinctual terror in my heart. Bakugo's scent is that of a predator, and I mustn't allow myself to succumb as his prey.

"Huhh?"

A small blessing; freezing on the spot was the optimal move, as Bakugo now sails overhead, propelled by his own ferocious momentum. I take off once more at full speed, desperate to escape the boy.

"Why, you..."

"No explosions, Kacchan! You'll hurt the little guy!"

"I won't, so shut up!"

"Plus, rabbits have a tough time dealing with stress! If something freaks them out enough, they can stop eating and be dead in a day!"

"Whoever designed this annoying animal did a

crappy job!"

All creatures can be annoying, humans included! We must inhale and exhale, eat and defecate, and sleep and awaken at frequencies that border on the absurd. I concoct this counterargument in my mind as I flee, failing to notice an object straight ahead. Unable to skid to a halt in time, I crash, producing a racket and...a foul odor?

"Damn rabbit, knocking over the trash we just spent all that time gathering up!"

Fool! It was not I who chose to place the garbage in this spot!

"Calm down, Kacchan..."

"Shut! Up! I've had enough of you bossing me around!"

While the children have their spat, I make a beeline for the elevator. Another pair of jumps and hasty button presses have me on my way. The doors open, but a distinct lack of Koji's scent tells me I have not reached

the third floor. Nevertheless, I must hide. I rise up on my haunches and sniff at the air, hoping to discern something, anything, about my surroundings. I detect a particular scent from one direction—the scent of paper. Following it, I discover another door left ajar. I enter cautiously. The paper scent wafts from prodigious stacks of magazines that occupy much of the room, as well as from the posters that plaster its walls. For my hiding place, I choose the gap between two of the stacks, and there I wait with ears pricked up and alert. No sounds. The two boys are not in pursuit. Perhaps they have occupied themselves with the scattered garbage. The curtains are shut, so this room is dim, though not entirely dark. My heart calms at last.

Free from mortal danger for now, I begin grooming to rid my coat of the stench and detritus I have picked up on my romp. This gives me time to reflect on the boy known as Bakugo.

He is unmistakably a predator, with a crude and foul mouth to match. That I should be forced to occupy the same space as this violent human is unthinkable. Suddenly, my mind's eye shows me a horrifying image: that of Bakugo hoisting a rabbit by its ears, which are

vital organs and literal bundles of nerves. People who handle us in that manner tend to be hunters.

Bakugo and gentle Koji could never see eye to eye, of that I am sure. And what if Bakugo should ever lash out in anger at my owner? Too distracted by my idle thoughts to continue grooming, I cower in place, frozen once more. I must protect Koji. Could I, though, should the need arise? Full of overwhelming fear, my heart threatens to leap from my chest.

I hear the elevator doors open.

"I'll check the fifth floor and work down from there, okay?"

"Less yapping, more rabbit hunting."

The doors close. I hear approaching footsteps. The sharp cluck of a tongue. Bakugo is coming.

I am paralyzed by fear as he advances down the corridor. Within moments, he notices the cracked door.

"Do any of these idiots know how to close a door?"

He throws the door open without a hint of reserve and stomps into the room, and my heart feels as though it has shriveled to a point. He will inevitably discover me in hiding, cruelly lift me by my ears, and add insult to injury with a triumphant sneer.

Bakugo stops and surveys the room.

"Ugh, we oughta burn this room to the ground with him in it!" he says. The disgust in his voice would be appropriate had he stumbled upon a writhing nest of centipedes.

It is not arthropods that fill the room, however. Only posters of naked female humans and magazines whose covers feature similar humans clothed in little to nothing at all. That boys this age would possess healthy sex drives seems perfectly natural to me. Instinctual, even. Bakugo's revulsion tells me, however, that the contents of this particular room imply lust bordering on unnatural obsession.

I gasp to myself. This is my opportunity to escape Bakugo's clutches. I screw up my courage and leap boldly from the magazines.

"Whoa! Oh no you don't... Ack!"

The piles of magazines collapse like an avalanche about Bakugo's feet, and by the time he falls to the ground, I have already dashed into the corridor. My savior, the elevator, awaits.

UA

"Kacchan? Didja find Little Yuwai?" said Midoriya.

"Not another word!" spat back Bakugo.

Izuku Midoriya had been searching the third floor, but the commotion from below had prompted him to check on how Katsuki Bakugo was doing on the second. He arrived just as a raging Bakugo stormed out of Minoru Mineta's room. Midoriya realized that the pet rabbit must've slipped through Bakugo's fingers, and though he said nothing further, Bakugo knew he knew.

"Got something to say?" said Bakugo, making an implicit threat. Midoriya forced a pained smile.

"No, but we've sure got our hands full, huh? And we'll never finish cleaning the place at this rate."

Bakugo seemed to agree as he scowled in silence, but a moment later, his lip curled into a sneer.

"We could always try that."

UA

How much time has elapsed since my daring escape from Bakugo? I cannot say, but I now sit in a shadowy corner of the first floor, catching my breath. I would hide forever if I could, but alas, that is not a real option. They pursue, and I, in turn, am pursued. It is a zero-sum game.

There exist hierarchies in all things, and within ours, I find myself at the bottom. I know full well that triumph in battle over a human such as Bakugo is quite impossible, but I should like to have him taste some small form of defeat at my paws nonetheless. If I can evade capture until Koji returns, I shall consider it a victory. It will feel as if I have somehow protected Koji from Bakugo…

Suddenly, an ambrosial scent fills my nose. I know it. Banana!

Banana! Banana! Where is the banana? My mind is dominated by the banana, as would the mind of any fortunate soul who has ever partaken of its soft, delectable flesh. Banana! Yes, banana! My sense of self is lost—there is only banana. Koji has given me banana on but a handful of occasions, yet it has been enough times that my instincts are tuned to it. Why must the banana be so delicious? Banana! Banana!

My legs propel me toward the scent. Every moment

that I am not feasting on the banana feels an eternity! My capacity for coherent thought dissolves, leaving only banana! Banana! Banana! Banana! Banana! Banana!

Every banana stepana brings me banana closer banana to the banana scentana banana banana!

At last, the banana!

My teeth tear into the fruit, and I feel myself go limp in ecstasy as its sweet flesh melts in my mouth. A pair of hands grip my body.

"You gave us a run for our damn money, furball..." says Bakugo with the triumphant sneer that haunted my earlier vision. Beside him, Midoriya smiles, sighs, and says, "Phew. Glad that's over."

I was lured by the banana and captured? The indignity of it all. I glare at my captors, these underhanded children who would dare use a banana as bait! No, I cannot fault them. A bout is a bout, and I have lost to them and their heavenly banana... I am not fit to protect Koji from the evils of this world.

"Hmm? Little Yuwai got so quiet... I hope he's not sick or something!"

"Ugh, you gotta be kidding me!"

UA

At the sound of rushed footsteps, I bound over to the door in anticipation.

"L-Little Yuwai..."

Koji! Welcome home! How many hours has it been since we last met? With joy in my heart, I leap into my owner's arms, but he holds me aloft and inspects my body with a look of grave concern on his face. Once satisfied that nothing is amiss, he sighs in relief.

"Well? Is Little Yuwai okay...?"

The question comes from Midoriya, who now stands outside the door with Bakugo. Still embracing me, Koji turns to the pair and nods.

"Thank goodness. The little guy just kinda went limp before, so we weren't sure."

"Great! Next time, trying giving a damn about your animal!"

Bakugo's cutting remark lingers in the air as he stomps off, and Koji seems to shrink, convinced that he is fully to blame for forgetting to shut the door this morning. For this, I am sorry, Koji. It was largely my

doing, and I hope that it does not weigh on you.

"Little Yuwai sure is clever, though," says Midoriya. "I was blown away when I realized he was using the elevator."

Midoriya says this to cheer up my owner, though his words seem to me to be genuine. Koji smiles and nods.

"Oh, right! We're collecting everyone's trash, so leave yours just outside your door, okay?"

Midoriya passes Kaminari and Ojiro as he departs and instructs them about the garbage as well before making for the elevator. Kaminari's gaze turns to me, and he grins.

"Didja escape again, Little Yuwai? You're one slick customer."

"I guess you forgot to shut your door tight?"

Your mild chiding ought to be directed at me, Ojiro. I suddenly feel the urge to leap at the boy's exquisite tail, but as I have caused Koji enough trouble for one day, I restrain myself. If Koji should grow sick from stress, I do not know what I would do.

"It's kinda hilarious to imagine, though," says Kaminari, plainly delighted by his own thoughts.

"Imagine what, exactly?" asks Ojiro.

"Those two, chasing this little guy around all day. I bet they were arguing the whole time."

Ojiro smiles awkwardly and says, "Yeah… I can definitely picture that."

Still convinced that he is to blame, Koji winces once more. I would that I could turn to him and speak.

Koji, I would say. *Those two boys get on better than you all suspect. They even expressed concern over my subdued condition upon capture. Bakugo may sport a foul mouth, yet he showed me a degree of kindness I could not have imagined, and he never once lifted me by the ears.*

Animals have something of a sixth sense for first impressions. A single whiff of a human's scent or the manner in which they touch us is often enough to inform us of their innate character. The wicked ones may wear cheerful masks and exhibit false compassion, but still they are wicked. Conversely, even a foulmouthed, ill-tempered boy may hold kindness in his heart. It may be an overstatement to describe Bakugo as kind, but surely he is not wicked. To this point, despite the cautiousness I exhibited in the pet shop, I could tell from a glance that you, Koji, were a person of upstanding character.

In any case, after my capture, Bakugo held me gently and brought me to your room. The two boys granted me the remainder of the banana in question and appeared relieved as I tore into it with gusto.

"Anything with an appetite like that ain't sick," said Bakugo.

"You're probably right," said Midoriya. "One time, when I was little, I tried to catch a stray cat using sardines as bait. It didn't work, so this feels like an especially satisfying victory."

Midoriya smiled as he indulged in this moment of nostalgia. I heard a curt cluck of Bakugo's tongue, and although I could not see his expression, I suspected that he too could appreciate such memories. My animal instincts do not lie.

Humans say that pounding rain hardens the ground, a metaphor that suggests, in this case, that from earnest conflict can spring forth some degree of mutual understanding. Well, perhaps their ground did not quite harden, but at the very least it turned to pliable mud, ready for reshaping.

As Midoriya went about the rest of his cleaning duties, he was sure to attend to me throughout the day. Midoriya is a considerate human. Bakugo inspected me once, as well.

Do you understand, Koji? You needn't worry. I may lack the strength to protect you, but this environment is a safe one. So please, attend to your daily studies with peace in your heart. You've much to learn if you hope to grow into a dashing hero, but I will await your return to the room for the rest of my days.

"Hmm? Why's Little Yuwai squeaking and grunting?" asks Kaminari.

"Aw, how cute is that!" says Ojiro.

Curses. If only these humans would invent a device capable of interpreting animal speech. Koji speaks to me in my crestfallen state.

"Little Yuwai, do you want to play outside...?"

No! But also, yes, more than anything! What keen intuition, Koji!

"Should be okay to let him loose in the courtyard, right?"

Ojiro, you magnificent creature!

Koji carries me to the first floor, where we spy Midoriya and Bakugo collecting the garbage, as promised. Mineta appears to be taunting Bakugo.

"Getting used to your new dirty job? Might as well

give up on hero stuff and shoot for the world's number one janitor!"

"How 'bout I light your room on fire, huh? That'll sure clean it up!"

Ashido and Uraraka enter the building, and my presence puts smiles on their faces. These two girls are prone to excessive petting, but as I am no petulant kit birthed yesterday, I do not resist their advances. No, they are not wicked souls, so I indulge them this pleasure.

"Unf, that floofy fluffiness soothes my soul," says Ashido.

"Going out to play in the courtyard? What a treat!" says Uraraka.

As the girl says, Koji! Quickly, now!

At last, Koji opens the door to my long-awaited paradise, and I breathe deeply, filling my nose with the fresh scent of grass. Behind us and across the space, the front door opens.

"Whew, long day!" comes a voice, prompting others to say, "Welcome back." I, too, would add to the chorus had I a voice to speak with. Yes, this space that I share with my new family is welcoming indeed.

Long, long ago, the demon lord conquered the world. Stripped of the will to fight back, the good people were oppressed and exploited by the wicked ruler, and long did they suffer under evil's reign. As it happened, a group of brave men and women found the courage to stand up against the darkness and despair. Heroes, they were called, and the greatest among them—All Might—smashed the demon lord back from whence he came, restoring peace to all the land.

These heroes were revered by all, and one boy from the countryside named Izuku held in his heart an admiration for All Might that bordered nearly on madness.

"Mother! I'm off to become All Might's apprentice!" said the boy, one day.

"Oh? Be careful, out there in the world," said his mother.

Though the mother was taken aback at her son's sudden, gleeful departure, she nonetheless saw him off with a smile and a wave. The boy's fanaticism had been apparent from an early age, so she knew there was nothing she could do when one of these moods gripped him.

The day before, Izuku had discovered a doll resembling All Might while walking through the woods, and that night, the great hero had come to the boy in a dream and proclaimed, "Lad! You can become a hero! A *fantasy* hero, that is!" The excitable Izuku had interpreted the dream as no less than prophecy, and so he now set out to meet his idol.

In high spirits, Izuku skipped down the road toward the town where he hoped to find All Might, but the boy soon lost his way. This was, after all, his first journey away from his own village. Fortunately, the lost, troubled boy was soon spotted by a positively Uraraka-looking girl named Ochaco and a boy clad in full armor named Tenya. When Izuku informed the pair of his quest for All Might, their faces darkened.

"They say that All Might has gone missing," said Tenya.

"What? How could that be?" said Izuku.

Rumor spoke of scores of heroes vanishing within the Realm of Sumwere, including All Might himself. Tenya, who came from a long line of proud knights, had set out to solve the mystery, and Ochaco had accompanied him as the mercenary mage employed by his family. Given the nature of their quest, Izuku decided to join them.

However, the road to Sumwere was long indeed, and the trio soon ran low on provisions.

"How odd... I was positive I had packed enough food for this trip..." said Tenya.

"Ah, sorry!" said Izuku. "We probably ran out cuz you're sharing with me now."

"Nonsense. I brought extra in case of emergencies, so we shouldn't have run out so quickly... Hmm? Ochaco, why do your cheeks bulge like a pair of rosy, waxing moons?"

"*Gulp*. Sorry! Using magic spells makes a girl hungry!"

"Hang on, can't you just create more food with magic?" asked Izuku.

"If it was that easy, you think I'd be busting my butt as a mage for hire?" said a peeved Ochaco, whose family finances made even peasants seem wealthy.

"Oh, right. Guess not. Sorry," said Izuku.

The trio trudged wearily on with empty bellies until they came across a tree bearing magnificent fruit. Grateful for nature's bounty, they plucked the fruit and began to eat.

"Oh, how absolutely scrumptious!" declared Tenya.

"It's all soft like mochi, with hints of *kinako* and brown sugar!" said Izuku.

"This'd go great with a nice cup of dirt tea! Boy, I wish Mom and Dad could taste this stuff!" said Ochaco.

The children were too busy stuffing their faces to notice a pair of guards approaching—guards clad in armor adorned with flame patterns.

"Was it you three who dared to steal Lord Endeavor's *kuzumochi* fruit?"

"Those who eat of the fruit face execution!"

The trio ran from the guards in a panic but soon found themselves cornered at a cliff's edge. Before the guards could make good on their threat, a boy appeared behind them.

"Leave them alone."

"Master Shoto! You may be our lord's heir, but we are not subject to your whims!"

"Shut up and get out of my sight."

Despite their protests, the guards followed Shoto's command, and the three travelers thanked their savior.

"I didn't do it for you. Just to get back at my rotten father," he spat with a scowl.

Shoto's father, Endeavor, was the notoriously ill-tempered lord of this province, where the rare kuzumochi trees grew. Those fruits happened to be the lord's favorite snack.

"That bastard's obsession with his precious trees drove my mother away. If he loved the trees so much, why not marry them, right…? As his heir, I'm supposed to keep the trees growing, but I'll be damned if I follow his plans for me."

Shoto might as well have been speaking of long-planned revenge for a loved one, such was the spite and enmity that pervaded his rant. Izuku and his companions took pity on the boy.

"Um, we're off to search for All Might and the vanished heroes. Want to come along?"

"Sure," answered Shoto in haste, eager for any excuse to remove himself from his father's shadow.

With that, the three travelers bound for Sumwere became four. However, they quickly lost their way and found themselves surrounded by crags in the foothills of a volcano on the verge of erupting.

"Ochaco!" cried Ida. "Can your magic aid us?"

"I'll give it a shot. Flame, frame, ram, and ramen, if here be fire daemon, show us the way, man!"

She drew her wand in a flash and pointed to a path through the heat and smoke.

"Should be this way!"

"Was that even real magic?" asked Shoto doubtingly.

The travelers nonetheless followed Ochaco and her wand until a plume of flame burst upon the path before them.

"You dare trespass on Lord Katsuki's volcano? You four got a death wish or something?"

The menacing, unyielding voice came from a shirtless boy cloaked only in a wild cape of fur. His mount was a red fire-breathing dragon.

"If you're hoping to pass, you gotta beat me in battle!"

"Defeat a dragon tamer...?" said Tenya. "Impossible! Let us beat a hasty retreat!"

"Running scared? Not on my watch!"

With that, the boy signaled his dragon to leap over the fleeing youths and block their escape.

"You totally shall not pass unless you take me down first!" said Katsuki with a fierce, indomitable grin.

"Looks like we're in for a fight," said Shoto, striking a battle-ready stance. Beside him, Izuku stared at Katsuki, pondered for a moment, and gasped.

"Hang on... You're Kacchan, aren't you? We used to be neighbors!"

"Huhh? Ugh, if it ain't Deku!"

"Wow, this brings back memories! How are your folks doing?"

"Just freaking fine and dandy! Thanks for asking, pleb!"

Upon realizing that Izuku and Katsuki must have grown up together, Tenya breathed a sigh of relief.

"Won't you yield to your childhood friend and his companions?" he asked.

"Nobody's yielding squat, cuz I've been waiting

my whole life for a chance to crush you, Deku!" said Katsuki.

"Crush me? But why, Kacchan?"

"You know exactly what you did!"

At Katsuki's seething words, Izuku gripped his lower lip and fell into thought.

"You mean, the time you wet the bed and tried to blame me, but then I told your mom it was actually you? Or that time we went cave exploring and I saw you get scared and turn tail? Or could it be how, when you were moving away, you gave me your prized possession, but I immediately dropped it and it shattered into a million pieces?"

"Yeah, all of that, peasant! So it's just you and me now, mano a mano, and you other merry fools better not interfere!" roared Katsuki with fiery rage. And so did their battle began.

"Seems like these two've got some history..." mused Ochaco.

The dragon blew jets of flame from the sidelines to fire up his warring master, and Izuku's companions cheered on their own champion. Locked in battle, the two boys barely paused to observe the volcano

erupting behind him. The goddess of victory smiled upon Katsuki that day, though, when his long-standing grudge exploded forth and gave him the slightest edge.

"Hah, this is my win!" he declared, standing proudly over a vexed Izuku. He turned to the other three and shouted, "Rules say you're all my servants now!"

"Huh?" said Ochaco. "What rules? You never mentioned any rules!"

"What the winner says, goes, you round-faced mage!"

"You are the clear victor, yes," said Tenya. "But we must venture on to the Realm of Sumwere to search for All Might and the vanished heroes!"

"Oh yeah? Tell me more."

After a brief explanation of the quest from Tenya, Katsuki's face turned pensive.

"I'm coming along," he said. "Anyone who can take down a buncha heroes has gotta be freaking strong. So I'll fight 'em, and I'll win!"

"Say what?" said Ochaco.

"You are welcome to join us, but journeying with your dragon may prove difficult..." said Tenya. But no sooner had he raised the issue than the red dragon transformed into a grinning red-haired boy, prompting shock and disbelief all around.

"Heya, I'm Eijiro the Half-Dragon. Part dragon, part human, y'know? If this form's fine with you dudes, then I'm glad to join the party!"

As it turned out, the brave and spirited Eijiro had been in service to Katsuki ever since losing a duel of his own.

With that, four travelers became six on the road to Sumwere.

The fellowship faced down all manner of beasts and demons, and after several death-defying days and nights over hill and dale, they at last arrived in the Realm of Sumwere. Instead of a bustling border town, however, they found only dusty streets, nearly devoid of residents.

"Where're the enemies?" shouted Katsuki. "Show yourselves!"

"Hmm… We'd better get some information before anything else," suggested Izuku.

In hopes of finding townsfolk to question, they made for the only tavern showing signs of life—the Dancing Tadpole. A charming girl with a froglike face greeted the six weary travelers.

"Welcome. We haven't hosted such a big group in quite some time. Please, call me Tsuyu."

Only two other customers were dining at the tavern—a sharp-eyed girl and a shifty man in a black hood. They did not sit together. When Tenya asked Tsuyu if she knew what had befallen the vanished heroes, the proprietress shook her head. She had seen the heroes arrive in town but could not say who or what had spirited them away. From one corner of the tavern, the sharp-eyed girl stared and listened intently.

"At the very least, the rumors were true," said Tenya. "I suppose we have no choice but to search every corner of the realm."

"How about some grub first, though!" said Eijiro.

The six travelers were glad for their first hot, cooked meal in some while, and they cleaned plate after scrumptious plate of food until they were fit to burst.

"What a delicious feast this was, Miss Tsuyu. How much do we owe you for it?" asked Tenya.

"That'll be thirty thousand Sumthins."

Tenya reached into his satchel for the money and froze. His face twitched, and he began to shake.

"What's up, Tenya?" asked Ochaco.

"We have no money! It seems a hole tore open in my satchel..."

"What? Everyone knows you gotta tie your purse strings tight and keep your bags well mended!"

"I apologize, but could you all pitch in to pay our bill?"

At Tenya's request, a dark pall fell over the party.

"Um, I've only got five hundred Sumthins on me," stammered Izuku.

"Money? Hah. I only believe in cold, hard barter. Like goods and services," said Katsuki.

"Sorry! Dragons ain't exactly known for carrying cash," said Eijiro.

"My employer's purse is all I've got. That means *yours*, Tenya," said Ochaco.

All eyes turned to their last hope—Shoto the lordling.

"Sorry, but you guys whisked me away after that business with the tree. I didn't bring my wallet."

With all hope lost, the travelers slumped in despair, pierced by Tsuyu's unblinking, uncompromising stare.

"Wait up, I bet we've got something to trade... Aww yes, here we go!" said Katsuki as he reached into Izuku's satchel and withdrew the All Might doll.

"Just sell off this All Might! It's gotta be worth something."

"Huh? No way! Give it back!" said Izuku, in an unusually resolute tone.

"That doll fills me with courage!" he said as he swiped it back. "The day I found it, All Might came to me in a dream and told me that with my stout heart and brave spirit, I could be a fantasy hero."

Izuku stuffed the doll—as precious to him as a piece of himself—back into his satchel.

"This's no time for your worthless dreams!"

"You're *not* taking All Might from me!"

While the boys' war of words escalated, the shifty man in the corner said, "Thanks," placed some money on the table, and left. The sharp-eyed girl, clearly deep in thought, watched him all the while. Then, from outside, came a piercing scream.

The party dashed out of the tavern and found it

surrounded by several dozen massive, red-eyed beasts with black wings sprouting from their backs.

"Are these...demons? But why here? Why now?" asked Izuku, always ready with a probing question or two, even in the face of mortal danger.

"Act now, question later," responded Shoto.

The beasts closed in on the party, but their travels in the wilderness had forged the six youths for just such life-and-death battles, and they quickly slew the creatures.

"Hah, was that s'posed to be a challenge?" howled Katsuki. "I'm hungry for more!"

"Relax, dude," said Eijiro, attempting to calm his companion.

"Hey, d'you think demon meat tastes good...?" asked Ochaco.

"I wouldn't try it, Ochaco. Their flesh would likely give you indigestion," said Tenya.

The sharp-eyed girl from the tavern had joined the fray at one point, and now she stood nearby, agog.

"You guys are wild..." she said.

As thanks for slaying the beasts, Tsuyu insisted that no payment for the meal was necessary and even offered the party a night's stay at the tavern. That evening, the

six enjoyed baths and clean beds for the first time in a great while, and they asked the sharp-eyed girl to join them. Her name was Kyoka, and she had been staying at the tavern for the past several days. Ochaco, in particular, was eager for conversation with another girl.

"So what do you do for work? Me, I'm a mercenary mage!"

"I guess you could call me a mercenary too," said Kyoka, but her every word seemed somehow evasive.

"Oh yeah? Then you know how rough this life can be! What do people hire you to do, exactly?"

"Well, this and that…"

"Lemme guess—you're a spy hired by the kingdom?"

"Huh? How'd you know?" said Kyoka, flustered by Ochaco's keen guess. She was, indeed, employed by the king himself, who, sensing the impending danger to the kingdom, had deployed spies to every realm in hopes of discovering whatever it was that now threatened the land. Upon learning that she and the travelers shared a common goal, Kyoka opened up.

"I'm thinking it might've been the demon lord who made all those heroes disappear."

"The demon lord himself? The one vanquished by All Might?" said Tenya in shock.

"That one, yeah," said Kyoka calmly. "His corpse was supposed to be buried deep underground, but at some point, it vanished, they say."

"Yikes…" said a stunned Ochaco.

"That would explain the demons we fought," muttered Izuku gravely.

"I suspect he's removing any obstacle that might keep him from rising to power again. And it's not just the heroes around here who keep going missing—it's gotten tough to find one anywhere nowadays," explained Kyoka.

The six companions gulped in fear. Who could say what might happen if the demon lord were to attack now, with no heroes remaining to defend the land? These youths had been born during the peaceful era following the defeat of the demon lord, but bedtime stories had taught them to dread him all the same. The air seemed to grow heavy around them as they imagined a return to the dark days they knew only from tales.

The door to their room swung open, and the man in the black hood stepped in.

"So it was you kids who slew those demons earlier?"

The man's shifty appearance put them immediately

on guard, until he removed his hood and caused Izuku to gasp in recognition.

"Long messy hair, five-o'clock shadow, scars under the eyes, and a neck wrapped in bandages…? You must be Aizawa the Hero!"

The rest of the group looked puzzled, so the delighted Izuku explained.

"He rarely shows himself, so there're rumors that maybe he doesn't even exist at all! But wow, what a treat to meet a real-life hero—here, of all places!"

Aizawa grinned at Izuku's exuberant introduction.

"Ever since the demon lord's revival, I've been searching for his lair in secret," said Aizawa. "I think I've found it, but if his influence has already spread this far, we've no time to lose. I mean to challenge him alone, but you, spy—get word back to the king. And the rest of you—can I count on you to help spread this news throughout the land?"

The fellowship was encouraged by this call to action. Katsuki, most of all.

"I've gotta be the one to slay the damn demon lord!" he said.

"Come now, we each have our roles to play in this

conflict! And on that note, we should depart, while the night is still young!" said Tenya.

As they rose from their beds and rushed out of the Dancing Tadpole, Aizawa placed a hand on Izuku's shoulder.

"Lend me that All Might doll. It may hold a clue of some sort."

"A clue? Well, trust me to find it, then! I know every last thing about All Might, including his bust-waist-hip measurements and even where to find those Yakushima cedar trees he loves so much!" said Izuku with stars in his eyes, nearly snorting in excitement. Aizawa heard him out in silence before letting loose a small sigh.

"Fine. But you're coming with me, then."

As the man and boy marched into the forest together, Kyoka watched from a distance with doubt in her eyes.

UA

"So you once fought alongside All Might? What's he like in real life? I heard he's drawn differently than the rest of us, even!"

A brief anecdotal war story from Aizawa had piqued Izuku's excitement once again, but the man now looked down at the boy with apathetic eyes.

"Oh, right, sorry!" said Izuku. He then hurriedly took the All Might doll from his satchel and inspected it by the light of the moon.

"So, this doll… I don't really notice anything weird about it… Hmm."

"No. You wouldn't," said Aizawa with a dry chuckle that sent a chill up Izuku's spine. He glanced up at the man, but nothing seemed amiss.

"Give it here."

"Oh. Sure…"

But just as Izuku extended the hand holding the doll, a mighty voice echoed in his mind.

You mustn't hand me over to him, lad!

"What was that…?"

"I said, give it here. Quickly, now."

"B-but…"

Caught between the voice in his head and his companion's outstretched hand, Izuku froze. Aizawa's listless eyes suddenly narrowed to icy slits.

"You shouldn't trifle with your betters, boy. Despite

my appearance, I'm no proponent of irrational killing, so you still have a chance to walk away with your life. Now… Hand. It. Over."

"Eek!"

The red flash in Aizawa's eyes was enough to force Izuku's legs to move, but before he could get away, the bandages around the man's neck uncoiled and lashed out like so many serpents. Izuku found himself bound fast in an instant.

"Why do you run? Aren't I one of the heroes you revere?"

"You…were… But something's not right, here…"

"I'll be taking that doll now."

"N-no! Wait!"

With a smug grin, Aizawa stuck a hand between the bandages and extracted the doll.

"What's so important about the doll…? Oh, wait! Are you just as big a fan of All Might as me? You should've said so sooner!"

"Not quite," said the man, all hint of levity gone from his face.

"You said All Might appeared to you in a dream? He

declared you a future hero...? Allow me to crush your prospects here and now."

"Urk!"

The bandages tightened around Izuku, but before the life could be squeezed out of him, a sudden burst of fire severed their connection to Aizawa.

"Thank goodness you still live, Izuku!" came Tenya's voice.

"You guys!"

Izuku freed himself from the loosened bandages and scampered over to his companions, including Tsuyu, Kyoka, and Eijiro in all his dragonian glory.

"I thought I told you lot to spread the word," said Aizawa, scratching his head in annoyance.

"Well, let's just say something seemed fishy," said Kyoka. "Because I heard that Aizawa the Hero was one of the ones who vanished... Meaning, you're probably not who you say you are."

"I'm afraid I am. However...I've been reborn as a demon!"

At this, a horde of fell beasts and demons emerged from the trees and surrounded the group.

"I would have let you live if only you'd followed my

commands... Sadly, there's only one rational way this can end now."

With a wide grin, Aizawa transformed into a hulking demon larger even than Eijiro in dragon form. The eight youths stared wide eyed at their towering foe, yet stood firm, ready to fight.

Tenya, Shoto, and Izuku leaped into battle, shouting and brandishing their blades. While they cut down one fiend after another, a roaring Katsuki tore through multiple foes at a time.

"Bring it on, punks!"

Eijiro's flames and bulk wiped out a good portion of the horde all at once. Nearby, the agile Kyoka fought with daggers, and Tsuyu used her unnaturally long tongue to fling attackers through the air.

"That's some tongue you've got, Tsuyu!" said a shocked Ochaco.

"I know. I spent some time with a circus, actually. My whole clan is blessed with this ability."

"Well, I'd better pull my weight too!"

With a full belly powering her spells, Ochaco's powerful magic blasts ripped through the ranks of the

enemy. Within moments, the companions had defeated every last demon save for Aizawa himself.

"It seems I underestimated you children. With the power you hold, why not join our side?"

"No thank you!" said Izuku.

"No way in hell!" echoed Katsuki.

Aizawa snorted at their blunt rejection and beckoned with one long claw—a clear provocation.

"No, I didn't think so. Have at me, then. Go on."

"Rahhhh!"

They rushed the demon, but their blades and spells couldn't pierce his hide. He retaliated with a series of swift attacks that belied his size. Though the youths refused to back down, victory soon seemed fleeting.

"What's the matter? Finished already?" said Aizawa, sounding almost bored.

Izuku and his companions fell to their knees, drained even of the energy to respond.

"It's time to end this, then," murmured their foe, his voice lacking all emotion. He lifted a massive leg, but before crushing Izuku underfoot, he stopped and spoke again.

"Ah, allow me to impart some knowledge as a

parting gift, because I'd hate for you to die thinking I'm a mere All Might fan... That doll you hold is none other than All Might himself, cursed into that pathetic form by the demon lord. A thieving bird carried the doll off, though, which is why I've been searching high and low for it."

At this, a voice echoed in the back of Izuku's mind... All Might's voice.

Lad! Like mine, yours is a pure heart that would seek peace for one and all. Now, become one with my power!

"Yes, All Might!" said Izuku, and he felt All Might's boundless energy flow into his body.

"Say goodbye... Huh...?"

Just as Aizawa brought his foot down, Izuku dodged out of the way. His companions gasped at the shimmering aura that now cloaked Izuku and his blade—an aura in the shape of the indefatigable All Might.

"I'm not finished yet... Because we've got a whole world to protect!"

"How...is this possible...?"

"Hahhh!"

With All Might's prodigious power filling his muscles, Izuku brought down his blade upon the demon.

"Tch… Gahhh!"

Struck down by the mighty blow, Aizawa's demonic body began to shrink. At the same time, All Might's power flowed back into the doll.

"Oh man, it's really you, All Might! I never dreamed that this'd be how I'd get to meet you!" said Izuku as he rushed to retrieve the precious doll.

Never mind me for now, lad—take a look at Aizawa. It was only the demon lord's curse that made him that way.

"Oh, right!" responded Izuku to the voice in his head.

As the group approached the felled hero with caution, his eyes blinked open.

"Hmm? Who're you kids?"

Aizawa had no memory of recent events, but after a brief explanation, he apologized for the trouble he had caused. According to him and the All Might doll, the demon lord had been cursing heroes, robbing them of their memories and transforming them into demons. Defeating the demon lord would break the curse and free the heroes.

"Meaning, the cursed heroes are likely to come after us now," said Tenya grimly. They all understood that the quest would only grow more dangerous.

"Fine by me!" said Katsuki with a bold laugh. "The only baddies worth battling are strong ones!"

"If you'll fight, then I will too! Besides, I can't just sit back while the world's in danger!" added Eijiro.

"This battle is mine as well! That means you're coming along, Ochaco!" said Tenya.

"No prob! We can discuss my fee later!" said Ochaco.

"I'm coming too! Gotta break this curse on All Might, at least! How about you, Shoto…?" said Izuku.

"Okay. Anything to put some distance between me and my bastard of a father," said Shoto.

"Don't forget me," said Kyoka. "I bet there'll be plenty of intel to pick up along the way."

"I'm coming along as well. My tavern is doomed unless we can restore peace to the world," said Tsuyu.

Aizawa stared at the enthusiastic youths and sighed.

"A positive attitude is great, but do you even know where to start looking?"

"Oh. Erm…" said Izuku. Aizawa sighed again.

"This quest is too dangerous for a bunch of kids on their own. Just stick me with."

The group cheered, thrilled to have found a trustworthy leader.

"Why do I suddenly feel like a schoolteacher...?" grumbled Aizawa.

His heart aflutter with high hopes for the quest ahead, Izuku spoke to the All Might doll.

"Once we break the curse...please make me your apprentice!"

Don't be foolish, lad—you're already my apprentice and then some! So don't let me down, now!

As the voice of the great hero echoed in his head, Izuku's face broke into a broad smile.

"Y-yes, All Might! I'll do my best! Oh, and when the curse is finally broken, can I get your autograph?"

Thus did the fellowship of ten brave souls venture forth, with all hopes set on the demon lord's defeat. But that, perhaps, is a tale for another time...

A Note from the Creator

I never thought we'd reach a third novel! This is
another rip-roaring fun one! I seriously feel blessed.

KOHEI HORIKOSHI